A SWEETHEART FOR ELIZABETH

A SWEETHEART FOR ELIZABETH

•

MAUREEN O'CONNELL

AVALON BOOKS
THOMAS BOUREGY AND COMPANY, INC.
401 LAFAYETTE STREET
NEW YORK, NEW YORK 10003

PRINTED IN THE UNITED STATES OF AMERICA
ON ACID-FREE PAPER
BY HADDON CRAFTSMEN, SCRANTON, PENNSYLVANIA

For my family,
For always believing

Chapter One

John Davis "Mac" McAllister hightailed it around the car, swung open the passenger door, and looked down into the biggest pair of blue eyes east of the Mississippi.

"Let's go, sweetheart. We've got just about five minutes to unload all this stuff before the game starts."

Reaching in, he unsnapped the restraining straps and scooped up into his arms twenty-three pounds and six ounces of wiggling baby girl. She answered him with a huge, drooling smile that showed off her very first two teeth and warmed him clear to his toes.

"And if we're really lucky," he continued as he carried her up the walk and into the house, ''that aunt of yours won't show up until our game is over.''

He patted the baby's bottom, checking on the state of her diaper, then plopped her into the mechanical swing that was set up in the living room. Winding it up, he gave it a push and hunkered down in front of her. ''Can't tell you much about her, Cappy. She kind of popped up out of the blue. Never even knew your dad had a sister. Or half-sister, I guess it is. And I'm sure he didn't know about her.'' Gurgling happily, the baby's tiny toes touched his chest as she swung toward him, then away again.

The aunt hadn't done much to enlighten him either. She'd simply stated, in a voice that didn't conjure up a very friendly face, that she'd only recently found out she'd had a half-brother. Then she'd offered her condolences for the accident, six months ago, that had taken not only her brother's life, but his sister's and parents' as well.

But if he'd been surprised to hear from Mike's long-lost relative, she'd sounded darn shocked when he'd told her about Cappy. A week later she'd called again, asking if she could come and meet her niece, and he'd agreed. Two days ago, a package had arrived from her for Cappy. He was still laughing. And the stuff was still sitting on one end of the din-ing-room table. Cappy wouldn't have much use, for a while, for a cardboard pop-up stage set with characters from Shakespeare's *Midsummer Night's Dream*, or four books suitable for a very precocious five-year-old, or the wood puzzles of dinosaurs, butterflies, and a map of the world. He guessed the kaleidoscope she'd included was for fun—if Cappy could have held it. He sure didn't want to prejudge the lady, but those were strange gifts to give to a baby who'd barely hit the half-year mark.

The tiny toes touched his chest again and he grabbed one gently between his fingers and gave it a squeeze. "I'm going out to the car to get the food, sport. So don't you go anywhere, all right?"

The baby made a sound like water sucked fast down a hole. No one could tell Mac she wasn't saying okay.

He took the porch steps in two easy strides. And no one could tell him that they weren't in for a pretty weird afternoon. He whistled for the dog as he sprinted to the car. She didn't come, which probably meant she was holed up in the house somewhere.

A car horn honked as he lifted a case of formula off the backseat. Three toots. Angie. She wasn't any too happy with him. He hadn't returned her calls for weeks. Maybe he would next week. Maybe—if she'd lay off the bit about his niece needing a mother. Placing the two sacks of groceries on top of the case of formula, he jogged up the steps and into the house.

Cappy burbled a welcome and flashed her uncle a fetching smile and he smiled right back.

Mac thought her the most beautiful baby girl the world had ever seen and he figured she was all the female he'd be able to handle for a long time to come.

Elizabeth Margaret Kincaid approached the porch stairs slowly. Too slowly. On purpose, actually—because suddenly she didn't know why in the world she'd decided to come to this North Carolina town in the middle of nowhere to call on a man who was the brother-in-law of a half-brother she'd never known and a child who was her half-niece, which made her a half-aunt . . . if there was such a thing!

Oh, yes, you do know why you're here, Elizabeth, she reminded herself sharply. *You know exactly why. Duty.* Filial duty. Prompted by a tear-filled, overseas telephone call from her mother. Her mother's muddled conversation was more of a confession, really.

And don't kid yourself, she thought. It was filial rescue, that's what it was. Again. After she'd promised herself that the last time was really going to be the last time.

She raised the tarnished brass knocker and rapped twice. And to be perfectly honest, she thought wryly, it had been her idea, not her mother's, to come here in person. Given the bizarre circumstances, she'd thought it the most appropriate thing to do. Though now, standing on the porch with the sun sticky hot on her back and a cramp in her leg from the drive, it seemed an incredibly impulsive decision and the feeling it gave her was about as pleasant as an ulcer.

She knocked again more sharply, and got no response. Not that she expected one—nothing, she realized with a flicker of annoyance, could possibly be heard over the awful blare of a television and the intermittent shouts of a deep, male voice.

The voice had to belong to him, of course— the brother-in-law. Coach Mac McAllister. A high school football coach, he'd told her. A jock, she'd told herself. The kind of man she'd sworn to avoid since she'd left her mother's house over ten years ago. Her mother's taste had been for the pros—football, baseball, tennis, and once, a race-car driver with a penchant for overturning his machines. They'd all shared a common denominator—careers on a downhill slide, and her mother's money as a lovely cushion. As far as she was concerned, though, a jock was a jock was a jock—and that included high school coaches.

She dropped her hand to her side and stared at the door. It needed paint. Badly. As did the rest of the small house. Her frown and the slight shake of her head were involuntary. The disapproval was not. She believed in doing whatever you do extremely well, and this place seemed a rather pathetic advertisement for a man who'd told her he painted houses during summer vacations.

As for knocking again? It was useless. There was absolutely no way she'd be heard over all that racket. Of course, he wasn't expecting her for another hour and it was much too late now to wish she'd called ahead to warn him of her early arrival.

Feeling like a burglar, she reached for the doorknob and turned it gingerly. It didn't make her feel a bit better when the door swung right open. She entered the house feeling furtive and guilty and walked into a room overflowing with baby paraphernalia and in need of a good dusting. Following the sounds of cheering and booing, she tiptoed down the short hallway, then stopped abruptly. She had a clear view of the room ahead.

A man, Mac, she assumed, was sprawled on the couch, bare feet on the coffee table, a bowl of popcorn balanced on one knee and a baby on the other. Both of them were wearing baseball caps and neither of them noticed her standing there.

But the dog did.

It came at her straight over the couch, teeth bared and bristling fur raised along its spine. It was the most enormous beast Elizabeth had ever seen and she had absolutely no doubt that it was about to tear her limb from limb. Terrified, she stumbled backward, her eyes glued to the dog as it hit the floor.

"Hey, Coll, no!"

Still snarling, the dog came to a skidding stop not a foot from Elizabeth and then, with a meek-as-you-please whine, began to wag its tail. She didn't trust the dog's about-face behavior one bit.

"Sorry about that, but you really scared the pants off the old girl sneaking up on her."

Elizabeth didn't dare take her eyes off the dog. She was sure it was about to leap up off its haunches and have another go at her, but she wasn't about to let the man's remark pass. "I did not sneak. I knocked, but there wasn't any way to make myself heard over all the noise in here." Her voice was an unfamiliar croak that did nothing to convey her outrage.

"I guess we *were* getting a little carried away. It's been quite a game."

A little carried away? That was putting it mildly. But Mac's chuckle, deep and unrepentant, acted on her like laundry starch, stiffening her knocking knees and hardening her resolve to regain at least a semblance of control. She lifted her eyes and didn't like a thing she saw.

Not the baseball cap riding his nose, not the amused lift of his lip or the unshaven jaw, and definitely not the tattered shorts and bare feet.

"Come on in and sit down."

For a moment Elizabeth simply stared in disbelief, first at Mac and then at the dog who was now fawning at her feet. Surely he was joking. "I am not moving until that animal is locked up," she stated flatly.

"Shoot, Elizabeth, don't you worry about her. I promise you, she's as gentle as a lamb."

A lamb? The man was nuts, no question about it. The animal looked more like a descendant of some large and ferocious prehistoric beast. Elizabeth opened her mouth to insist that she was not going to budge as long as that animal was loose but Mac had already turned away from her and was strolling back into the room. The dog went too, without so much as a backward glance. Very reluctantly, she followed, and only, she reassured herself, because she was a guest in his house.

The dog settled down in front of the television as she perched warily on the edge of the couch. If she didn't know better, she'd have sworn the thing was watching the game.

"You are Elizabeth, aren't you?"

"Well, of course I—" Her mouth snapped shut abruptly as she turned to face him. He had a grin on his face as smug as a Cheshire cat's.

His baseball cap was tipped back and her niece was snuggled up against his chest.

"I was hoping you were, because I've kind of discouraged the ladies from dropping in unannounced."

Elizabeth stifled a groan. Bad enough the man was a jock—but a flirt too? Her lips pressed together in a thin line of forbearance as she pushed her glasses up more firmly on the bridge of her nose. It wasn't just going to be a long afternoon—it was going to be interminable.

Still grinning, Mac gave her a long, slow wink. "This little lady here takes up most of my time."

With a start, she looked guiltily at the baby all cozied up in his arms. Her niece was the sole reason she was here, and what with her sneaking in (which she didn't) and the dog and this man, she hadn't said as much as hello to the child.

The baby lay, all rounded and dimpled, against Mac's chest. A stab of longing, of something lacking, nearly took Elizabeth's breath away. The urge to reach out and touch the red-gold ringlets, the tiny hand, the button nose, was overwhelming, but it was too late. Incredibly, in spite of all the commotion, her niece was fast asleep.

Mac bent his head to the baby and traced his finger along the curve of her pink cheek.

"Guess you'll have to visit with her later, Elizabeth. She's definitely going to be out for a couple of hours." Standing, he hoisted the sleeping infant to his shoulder. "Just make yourself comfortable. I'll be right back."

Much to her relief, the dog rose immediately and followed Mac out of the room.

"And keep an eye on the game for me, okay?" he called back.

Elizabeth sank against the cushions, feeling oddly deflated though she was grateful for the few minutes' reprieve. Just how she was going to pass the time with this man while her niece was napping was a mystery to her. Her own world—orderly, reliable, and predictable— seemed light-years away.

She gazed around the room, puzzled by the empty bookcases, the blank walls, the lack of family pictures or bric-a-brac. It was as impersonal as a motel—maybe more so, given the fact that Mac lived here, that this was his home.

She heard him whistling somewhere in the house and flinched. The man had her nerves jangling like a bad alarm and her stomach was still roiling from the encounter with his dog. She stared vacantly at the television. He'd asked her to watch the game for him. Not a good omen. She'd seen a game once, at about eight years of age, in the company of a step- father who'd been part-owner of the team. That particular marriage of her mother's had lasted less than three months and she hadn't been in a ballpark since.

Straightening up, she set her purse on the cluttered coffee table, knocking a plump, plush teddy bear to the floor. Picking it up, she tried to ignore the small, sudden ache that spread unexpectedly through her chest. She'd never held a baby in her arms, she realized as she carefully set the bear back on the table. Not even once.

She shifted her attention back to the TV in an attempt to dispel the unfamiliar sense of inadequacy she felt. She was vaguely aware of the camera panning the crowd as they leaped to their feet, arms waving, mouths wide in roaring approval. But it was Mac she saw, bare feet planted wide, his head bent to the baby nestled against his chest. That male image was as foreign to her as the game he'd asked her to watch.

"I've brought you a Coke, Elizabeth. Now, why don't you kick off your shoes and relax?"

Mac's voice nearly brought her off the couch. Startled, she sucked in a breath, then clapped a hand to her nose, just barely stifling the urge to sneeze—and the urge to snicker. The man was covered in powder, from the neck of his faded T-shirt to the bottom of his cutoffs. He swiped at the stuff haphazardly, without a trace of embarrassment. The powder sifted onto the coffee table, layering the scattered popcorn in a dusting of white. Relax, he'd said? She took the can from his outstretched hand, murmuring her thanks. If she'd suddenly been plunked down on Jupiter, she couldn't have felt more out of her element. To relax was out of the question. Persevere was more like it. And she had absolutely no intention of removing her shoes.

"Well, now, Elizabeth, I'm glad to meet you finally." Mac settled himself down on the couch right next to her and took a good, long look at Cappy's aunt.

He had to admit that she was good-looking, if you liked your women cool and classy. It did help a bit though, he thought, that her eyes were the same cornflower blue as Cappy's and her hair just a shade or two darker than their niece's fiery mop. It didn't help, however, that those eyes, behind glasses he thought were too large but could tell she needed, held about as much warmth as a February freeze or that her hair was pulled spinster-tight in a knot at the back of her head. She was some kind of uptight lady, all right—and he didn't have the first idea just why she'd decided to visit them.

"It's nice to meet you too." Her reply was distracted. The dog had her worried; she realized she hadn't seen it return with Mac. Perhaps it was lurking behind the couch this very moment. She couldn't help glancing over her shoulder.

Mac couldn't help noticing. "If you're looking for Colleen, I put her outside."

"Colleen?" For the first time since she'd arrived, her smile was spontaneous. "That's the name of that, uh, your dog?"

"Yep. She's an Irish wolfhound and a friend of mine reminded me that Colleen meant girl in Gaelic, so we figured it would work."

"Oh." She thought the name worked about as well as calling a leprechaun Paul Bunyan, but she kept her mouth shut. She sat a little easier, though, just knowing the dog wasn't within striking range.

"So how's the game going?" He popped open the tab on his can of soda and took a long swallow.

"I really don't know."

Mac's head swiveled quickly to the television, then back to her again. "You don't know?"

"No, I don't." Now what? The man was looking at her as if she'd suddenly sprouted horns. "I'm sorry, but I don't know anything about baseball. I never watch," she added lamely.

For Pete's sake. Mac stared at her as if he hadn't heard correctly. What was to know? When he'd left the room, the bases were loaded, the hitter was warming up at the plate, and here she was telling him she didn't know what had happened. Worse yet, he could tell she was dead serious. Absently, he rubbed the palm of his hand along his faintly stubbled jaw. This little get-together wasn't going to be easy.

A bit of air whistled softly through Mac's lips and Elizabeth winced. She'd sounded too abrupt, maybe even rude. She smiled and nodded toward the television. "I didn't mean . . . Please, don't let me stop you from watching."

"Yeah, well . . ." He eyed the screen longingly. *Well, what, Mac? The lady's your guest. And you're not gonna enjoy the game anyway now.* Not with her sitting there looking about as comfortable as a cat at a dog show. Picking up the remote control, he pushed the OFF button. He'd give her a tour of the house and yard. That would eat up some of the time—not enough, probably—but it would get them moving. "Don't worry about it. I'll catch the scores on the news tonight."

Her jaw felt tight from the smile she kept on her face. He was sounding just a little too long-suffering.

"Please, Mac, I certainly don't want to interrupt your game."

"Hey, it's no problem." He rose quickly from the couch before he could weaken and take advantage of her half-baked apologies and turn the tube back on. "Come on. I'll show you around the place. I just bought it a couple of months ago and I'm still unpacking.''

That explained the barren, unlived-in look, Elizabeth thought as she followed Mac into the living room.

''Well, I'm sure it takes time,'' she murmured as she trailed after him through the dining area and into a kitchen that looked a lot more lived in than the rest of the house.

''I can handle the painting and cleaning,'' Mac said. ''But my sisters are going to have to give me advice on decorating the place.''

Elizabeth stopped dead in her tracks. Sisters? The word hung in the air as if it had taken physical form. She was stunned. He had sisters? Frowning, she fiddled with her glasses. Then what in the world, she wondered, was this man, this bachelor uncle, doing with the baby? ''You, uh, you have sisters?''

''Yeah. Kate and Mandy. They wanted me to tell you they look forward to meeting you.'' He held open a door that led to a screened back porch and motioned her through.

''Oh. Well, I—'' His answer wasn't at all what she expected and she found herself stammering in response. ''—I look forward to meeting them also.'' She inched her way around unpacked boxes, a bike, garden tools, and a baby carriage. There had to be a reason, she thought, that Mac had the baby. Perhaps they were out of the country. Surely there was a logical explanantion for this most peculiar arrangement. She bent to examine the carriage and asked as blandly as possible, ''Do they live in the area, Mac?''

''They sure do.'' Mac just barely kept himself from chuckling out loud as she jerked upright and faced him. The look on her face was as simple to read as a road map. Absolute astonishment. As the silence between them lengthened, he could practically hear the wheels turning. She couldn't figure out just how to ask the next question. He decided to make it easier for her.

''If you're like most folks, Elizabeth,'' he said as kindly as he could, ''I'll bet you're wondering why one of my sisters doesn't have the baby.''

Elizabeth had no conscious recollection of the last time she'd blushed, but there was no mistaking the feel of it now as the heat moved up her neck and spread to her cheeks. Subtlety certainly wasn't the man's long suit. She raised her chin and looked him directly in the eye. Well, she wasn't easily intimidated and she could be just as blunt. ''Frankly, yes.''

Mac was surprised at the blush. It was a minor inconsistency that didn't quite jive with his impression of her. But he sure wasn't surprised by her reaction. Most everyone seemed to think it strange. And it never failed to amuse him. His explanation was always the same and while truthful, not the whole truth. He didn't talk easily about love. He shrugged. "It's kind of simple, really. My sister Mandy is a single, working mom with two young kids. She has plenty on her plate. My sister Kate has five children and a husband who has to travel. Ditto for her. This arrangement seemed the best for all of us."

"Oh, I see." Elizabeth knew she'd didn't quite see, at all. She simply didn't understand him or his logic. In her circle of acquaintances, she knew of no man who would voluntarily take in an infant. As a matter of fact—

Her thoughts were interrupted as the house was filled with the shrill, high cry of a baby and a ringing phone.

Mac propelled them both back into the kitchen. "Would you mind getting the baby while I get the phone? She's in the bedroom to the left down the hall." He hustled out of the room without waiting for an answer.

Not that Elizabeth could give one. Even if a gun had been held to her head, she couldn't have spoken. She'd been struck mute, temporarily paralyzed with panic.

Chapter Two

Get the baby? Elizabeth's stomach took a nosedive to her toes. *No way!* Her adrenaline level shot up, along with a strong desire to flee. Pride forced her out of the room and down the hall.

She approached the door to the baby's room on tiptoe, trying to muster up the courage to enter. Get the baby, he'd said to her—casually, confidently, never suspecting. *How can it be,* she thought wildly, *that I've lived twenty-eight years and never so much as picked up a child?* There were reasons, good reasons—she knew that—but not a single one of them consoled her as she entered the room and edged slowly toward the crib.

18

It was silly to tiptoe, for it wasn't as if her niece could possibly hear her. Elizabeth couldn't imagine how something that size could make that kind of noise. When she bent over the crib and saw the scrunched, red face and the flailing arms and legs, she almost screamed herself. There simply had to be something terribly wrong with the child. But Mac hadn't even hinted that this might be an emergency, and he'd certainly assumed she'd know what to do.

Reaching down, she slid her shaking hands under the infant's arms and slowly began to lift her. What surprised her first was the weight. Caroline looked as light as goose down but felt as heavy as a fattened goose, Elizabeth decided as she carefully inched her up and over the rail. And what really scared her was the infant's wiggling energy. Her grip tightened and she whispered to the baby frantically, begging her to hold still. The wiggling didn't stop and the screeching seemed to get louder.

"Oh, Caroline, please." She backed up to the rocker sitting near the crib and lowered herself into it, praying she wouldn't drop the child.

"Tell me you're all right," she begged. Somehow she managed to maneuver the baby into a sitting position, but Caroline's head was bobbing alarmingly and she was still sobbing. Elizabeth thought of calling for Mac to come help but couldn't bring herself to do it. She would, she thought grimly, find a way to comfort the child before he came back.

Mac stood in the doorway watching her, unobserved, and thought he hadn't seen a sorrier sight in his life. A woman who didn't even know how to hold a baby! She had Cappy at arm's length, sitting way out on her knees, and the way she was talking to her sounded every bit as awkward as the way she was holding her. But there was something in the tilt of her head, and the desperate pleading with the baby to tell her what was wrong, that got to him. She seemed almost as vulnerable—and as miserable—as the kid.

Striding into the room, he plucked Cappy off Elizabeth's lap and settled her on his shoulder. To let this continue would be nothing short of torture for the two of them.

"Now what's the matter, sweetheart?" A few firm pats on her back gave him the answer. Cappy made a loud and very impolite burp and then buried her face in his neck. "It was the apple juice," he explained.

Elizabeth didn't know when she'd felt so grateful—or so stupid—so she grabbed at his explanation like a lifeline. "Oh, yes, the apple juice. Of course, I wasn't really sure. She seemed in such distress."

"Well, don't you worry. This little tyke yells like a banshee when she has gas pains in her tummy. She just needed a good burping."

Elizabeth had taken off her glasses, and Mac noticed for the first time that her eyes were shaped just a tad differently than those on the sweet-smelling bundle in his arms. They had more of a tilt to them that gave her a slightly exotic look. And the way she was staring at the baby, with a frightened yet yearning expression, got to him. For all her stiff-necked ways, he felt an urge to pat her on the shoulder, let her know he didn't hold it against her for going to pieces, and tell her everything would be all right.

A second look at her stopped him cold. She'd put the glasses back on and her mouth was pursed up tight as a drawstring. He figured he'd guessed all wrong.

Elizabeth watched numbly as he settled the baby back in the crib. She couldn't think of a time when she'd felt so inept. Mac had taken Caroline from her and quieted her down in something like microseconds. And then he'd looked at her with such awful pity—or was it reproach? She wasn't sure. All she knew for certain was that she wouldn't win any popularity contest with these two. And she was surely weary of Mac telling her not to worry.

She shoved at her glasses, stood up stiffly, and gazed down at Caroline. The baby stared back at her as if she too had serious doubts about her aunt. After all, who wouldn't know when a baby needed burping? Anyone would, Elizabeth thought bleakly as she watched her niece's eyes flutter closed and a tiny thumb head for her mouth. Anyone but her.

Elizabeth jammed the gearshift into first and stepped down on the accelerator so hard the car sprayed gravel as it left the curb. Embarrassing, of course. She shifted carefully into second. But given her state of mind and the events of the last few hours, her embarrassment took a definite backseat to her overwhelming relief at leaving. Later, much later, she would try to sort out just what had gone wrong. Not what, she thought grimly, but how much. And why.

She caught a final glimpse of the two of them in her rearview mirror just before she turned the corner. The image lingered as she braked noisily to a halt at one of the few stoplights in the town: a man in a baseball cap holding a baby with hair the color of the setting sun.

She reached the interstate, flipped on the cruise control, and shoved a tape in the stereo. The soothing music of one of her favorite string quartets filled the car. If nothing else, she was headed home, and she was grateful, so very grateful. . . .

*　　*　　*

Mac stood on the sidewalk, the baby riding his hip, and grinned as he watched the car bolt from the curb. ''She's going to peel some rubber, Cap.'' He chuckled. ''I wouldn't have thought she had it in her.''

The baby yawned hugely and closed her eyes. When she was tired, not even a straight-laced aunt peeling rubber could keep her awake.

Mac shifted the baby from his hip to his arm and cradled her against his chest. ''Okay, sport. Bedtime.''

He tucked her into her white wicker crib, all trimmed in lace and ribbons, pulled the pink and white comforter up to her nose, then touched the mobile hanging above her. Tiny baseballs, mitts, and bats tilted and spun as he bent and kissed her cheek.

''That aunt of yours, Cap,'' he whispered to the sleeping baby, ''sure ruined a great game.''

But their team had won. Good thing, he thought as he flipped out the light. He and Cappy had two bucks riding on it. As for that aunt of hers . . . well, they'd scored somewhere around zero with her. But he had a hunch about that lady. There wasn't a way in this world she had a man in her life.

Mac shoved open the door of his aging **VW** bug, smacking his kneecap, as usual, on the steering column as he swung his long legs out. It barely caused a wince—until his bare feet hit the ground and sizzled, like two fried eggs, on the hot asphalt.

"Ow!" he yelled, jerking his feet up a couple of inches and reaching for the pair of tennis shoes he'd thrown on the floor. Shoving his feet into shoes that looked as if they'd been around longer than his car, he ducked his head and slid out. He slammed the door shut so hard, it rocked the car like a cradle. It was one indication of his mood.

Stalking toward the motel entrance, he kept wondering just what in the world Elizabeth was up to now. Ever since she'd blown into town a month ago, like some kind of arctic wind, she'd been driving him crazy. Twice-weekly phone calls, multiple questions, and now she was back again, summoning him into her presence like royalty.

He swung open the heavy glass door. Okay. He'd admit she had reason to keep in touch. Cappy was her niece too. And he wanted to have kindlier feelings toward the lady. Really. But her type wasn't his cup of tea at all.

He nodded absently at the young woman wiggling her fingers at him from behind the reservation desk. Normally, he'd have done a lot more than nod—if his mind hadn't been fixated on the lady waiting for him.

He figured he had her pegged pretty well by now. She was one of those career women who'd put their romantic notions on ice, their biological clocks on the back burner, and their life on a drill sergeant's schedule. Not the kind of woman he'd been accustomed to going out with. Not that he had time for any woman these days. Not that he even wanted to make time, for he'd given his heart to a little lady with Orphan Annie hair and the smile of an angel.

The elevator door closed on him with a soft whoosh, bearing him upward in a richly paneled cocoon that smelled faintly of spice.

The hotel was brand spanking new and a pretty fancy place for his small town. There were two other motels that'd been in the area longer than he could remember, but they were mom-and-pop affairs—long on friendliness and short on the amenities this place could offer. He guessed the Sheraton chain was willing to take a gamble because of the loop of interstate, the trickle of water they called a river in these parts, and the dreams of the town council.

And he couldn't quite imagine Elizabeth staying anywhere but here.

He took his time walking down the thick carpeted hallway. He knew the only reason Elizabeth wanted to meet with him was because of Cappy. Their niece was the only tie between them, the only thing they had in common. He tugged at the bill of his baseball cap, pulling it lower on his forehead. The vibes he was getting weren't good. He didn't trust the lady—not a whit. By the time he reached her door and raised his hand to knock, he was primed and ready to deal with Ms. Elizabeth Margaret Kincaid.

Elizabeth paced the two-room suite, stopping, for the sixth time in as many minutes, to rearrange the throw pillows on the couch. It was perfectly understandable, she reassured herself again, to feel slightly nervous, slightly stressed. Motherhood had never been on her agenda.

She reached the window and pulled open the drapes, flooding the room with mid-July sun, and checked her watch. Fifteen minutes late. No surprise there. The man wouldn't be worried about something as mundane as punctuality. He was a jock. That, for her, explained everything. Well, almost everything. She retraced her steps, circling the couch. To be absolutely fair, it wasn't that he was an unsuitable guardian for Caroline. He was doing the very best that he could. She knew that. And his sisters seemed to have no problem with the arrangement. But how could they? How could he? They'd had no other options. Until now.

She stopped before the credenza and stared at the picture of Caroline that Mac had given her. Something knotted in her throat. There'd been times when she'd called Mac and heard Caroline shrieking with delight in the background and twice Mac had asked her to speak up so he could hear her over ''his noisy bunch of relatives.'' When she'd hung up, the silence had been loud. She'd turned on the television and it hadn't helped—it hadn't drowned out the sounds of family.

She had family, of course, if you wanted to count the succession of stepfathers she'd met infrequently when she'd been let out of boarding schools and camps. All of that was a long time ago—and she felt nothing but pity now for her once-glamorous mother whose fading beauty and lack of a current husband had sent her into voluntary seclusion at a chateau in the south of France.

She knew that her mother's dependence on men was a large part of the reason she'd never felt the least urge to marry—or become a mother, for that matter. She'd pursued her education and career, driven by the need to feel useful—to *be* useful. It had been all-consuming and had filled all the empty places—or so she had thought.

She spun away from the picture and resumed pacing. From the day she'd met Caroline, she'd begun to dream. Dreams that stirred up feelings she could barely identify and dreams that haunted her waking hours, conjuring up images of herself and her niece. A walk down the street became an emotional mine field. There were babies everywhere: pushed in strollers, carried on backs, strapped to bicycles. Once, hurrying down a busy sidewalk, she'd seen a man in a baseball cap and cutoffs pushing an ornate and very English pram. It wasn't Mac. She knew it wasn't even as she followed the man for two blocks. Watching him disappear around a corner, she'd stood with her hands clutched against the ache in her chest until a woman had asked, in a voice edged with alarm, if she was all right.

The very next day she began to make the rounds to pediatricians, child psychologists, and her lawyer. She'd even spoken with a few acquaintances with children, people she'd traditionally avoided. The results had been clear. At least to her. Caroline needed her, needed what she could give to her. She was financially secure and in line for promotion to V.P. at her accounting firm. She could offer Caroline the best schools and the cultural opportunities her uncle could never provide for her. It never crossed her mind that Mac might not agree.

And she wasn't quite ready to listen to the small voice that whispered inside her, *Who needs whom, Elizabeth?*

When she heard the knock at the door, she took a deep breath and crossed the room. This time she was more than ready to deal with "Coach" Mac McAllister.

Elizabeth swung open the door with a polite smile on her face and didn't have one second to utter the welcoming phrases she'd thought would be appropriate. Instead, Mac pushed right by her as if she wasn't there and strode directly into the room.

"So what is it you wanted to see me about, Elizabeth?" His voice sounded belligerent as he spun to face her.

She closed the door slowly. She hadn't counted on this reaction. When she'd called and asked to meet with him, he'd sounded curious, maybe, but nothing more. Whatever he'd thought about her request to meet with her at the hotel, he hadn't expressed it. For that she'd been grateful. The telephone wasn't the venue she wanted for their discussion. Though she'd been acutely aware that they had no reason on earth to get together, other than Caroline, she simply couldn't believe he had a clue about her motives for this meeting.

Feeling suddenly on the defensive, she reminded herself that she had taken into account his attachment to the child. After all, he'd been around Caroline since the day she was born. But it seemed to her an impossible stretch of imagination to think a thirty-four-year-old bachelor would actually relish the idea of being a single father.

There were a couple of rules she adhered to when negotiations promised to be difficult:

Velvet gloves wouldn't bruise egos, and give time, time. She'd use them now. Her smile was magnanimous—and a mistake.

"Hello, Mac. Thank you for coming." She motioned toward the couch. "Won't you sit down?"

She was one cool dame. Mac lowered himself onto the couch with a grunt of thanks as Elizabeth took a seat on the chair opposite him. Too cool. Too controlled. He eyed her critically. Okay. She was looking good. Too good. No bun this time. Just a spill of that red-gold hair over her shoulder. And a spill of long legs too, he noticed, from a skirt that hitched up near her knees as she sat. He let his eyes linger an appreciative moment or two. All together she was a pretty nice package, barring her personality. That had about as much appeal as a Siberian winter.

"Would you like something to drink?" Elizabeth didn't like the way his eyes were roaming over her, from her head to her toes and back again and with the scowl still on his face. She stood up quickly and went to the small, well-stocked fridge. "There's soda, Perrier, and, uh, beer."

Mac leaned back against the cushions and stretched out his legs. He'd darn well heard her put just a shade too much emphasis on the beer. It was what she expected him to want and to ask for. A real "go-with-the-gusto" kind of guy. He decided to oblige the lady, even though he rarely drank the stuff. But he might as well let her think she had him figured out. "A frosty one sounds just right, Elizabeth," he said with fake heartiness.

"Would you like a glass?"

"Nah. A can's good enough for me." He almost chuckled out loud as he watched her mouth thin. He'd give her points for making no comment on his choice—she was a lady to the bone. When she took out his beer and reached for a Perrier, he couldn't help smiling. He'd have bet a grand, and won, that she'd choose that overpriced water in a bottle. She was one predictable female. He thumbed open the top of the beer can, took a sip, and set the can on the coffee table. He'd wait for her to make the next move.

Elizabeth settled down on the chair, smiled, took a sip of the Perrier, and asked how Caroline was doing. As he answered, she couldn't help but think how well she'd handled him. The scowl was gone, he seemed to be relaxing, and when he asked her again what she wanted, she heard herself say, "I want custody of Caroline."

The words hung in the air between them and for a long, drawn-out moment, they simply stared at each other.

Elizabeth couldn't believe what she'd just blurted out. She'd rehearsed, so many times, a scenario in which she would logically lead him to see what was so clearly evident to her. She could provide for the child far better than he. Caroline was going to need her as she grew older—she would need all the things Elizabeth could do for her. But now in the space of a few seconds, her plan of a reasoned, civilized discussion was in a shambles, ruined by words that had simply flown out of her mouth as if they had a mind and wings of their own.

''What?'' Mac croaked. He honestly thought he just might not have heard her correctly. ''Custody of Cappy? You mean custody, like you have her and I don't?''

Elizabeth made a small, self-deprecating sound and watched, with a growing sense of horror, as he hunched forward. His eyes, normally a smoke gray, were flinty and hard and bored right through her. His hands were gripping his knees. Boy, she'd really made him mad.

She clutched the glass she was holding so tightly, she thought it might crack and shatter. *Stay calm,* she told herself. *Stay very calm and say something, anything, to take that murderous look out of his eyes.*

Her voice, when she found it, was uncharacteristically shaky. ''I'm sorry. I simply wanted to discuss the, uh, unfortunate situation.'' She tried her most conciliatory smile.

"I'm sure both of us are concerned about Caroline's future."

Just the simple act of speaking helped, though she still couldn't seem to stop glancing at his hands. They were so very large, though why shouldn't they be? Mac was large. Six-foot-something, she guessed, of lots of muscle, and at the moment all that muscle looked very imposing.

Slowly, he began to relax. Elizabeth watched, breathless and with a kind of morbid fascination, as he leaned back into the cushions. She felt just a bit silly. He simply wasn't the type of man she was accustomed to dealing with and she'd overreacted. She brought the glass to her lips and took a shaky sip of the Perrier.

She'd shocked him, all right, Mac thought, with a curveball he'd never expected she could throw. But she'd also made him feel awfully peculiar. He couldn't recall a time in his life when he'd seen a woman with such alarm in her eyes. And somehow he was responsible for it, though he couldn't see how. But he didn't like it, not one bit. He could tell she was calming down now, and not just calming down, but getting that supercool, superior look about her again. And he didn't like that much either. But it beat the fear.

He rubbed one hand along his thigh and exhaled slowly. There wasn't any need for him to get riled up. What she suggested was so patently ridiculous, so crazy, it began to amuse him. The career lady, the upwardly mobile C.P.A. with her eye on a corner office, wanted to raise Cappy? He had to hide the smile that started to pucker his lips.

"Well now, Elizabeth," he drawled, "why don't you tell me about this plan of yours?"

She would've given just about anything to snatch her earlier words right out of the air, but the damage was done and she had only one choice left. She'd brazen it out and hope she could salvage something.

"Plan? Oh, no, Mac. There's no plan, as such. I don't have anything firm in mind." Her laugh sounded to her like the nervous titter of a teenager. She gritted her teeth in frustration. How *could* she have gotten herself put on the defensive like this? And by him, of all people? "It's all rather still in the thinking mode."

Thinking mode? Mode? Her choice of words was as strange as this little meeting she'd gotten up. And this was about Cappy? About a little tyke who wouldn't know the word mode from mom? Mac was beginning to feel sorry for Elizabeth—again, and against his better judgment.

But he wasn't about to let her off this particular hook that easily, not when it was about Cappy, about the love of his life. "Well, then, maybe you and I aren't speaking the same language, Elizabeth. I could have sworn I heard you say you wanted custody of Cappy.''

''This isn't a matter of wanting, Mac. It's what's best—best for Caroline. And I do want you to know, I think you're doing a fine job, an excellent job, with her. But I was looking ahead to her future. When she's a young girl and she's being raised by a man—not that fathers aren't perfectly capable, but you're not her father and I'm thinking long-term, of course—well, it just seemed more than obvious that I could be of great help to her. I mean I thought—''

Her mouth shut with a snap. What *did* she think? Her eyes skittered nervously away from Mac's unsettling gaze. She sounded garbled, nearly unintelligible. It was so totally unlike her she felt like a stranger in her own skin. It was Mac, of course. This man. She shifted uncomfortably in her chair. For reasons that simply baffled her, she couldn't seem to put two sentences together when she was around him.

It was happening again, Mac thought, this urge of his to wrap his arm around her and tell her she was just about as mixed up as anyone he'd ever met and he had a gut feeling she couldn't help it. But it was his Cappy she was talking about and she hadn't once mentioned the buzzwords that would've gotten his attention. Simple words like love and caring. She could be of help to Cappy? He didn't think that little dynamo was going to need anyone's help. But she would always need someone's love.

And then it came to him—a way to show Elizabeth that being a parent was a lot more than she'd bargained for. He felt just a tad guilty about taking advantage of that kind of naïveté but not enough to stop.

"Do you have any free time, Elizabeth? Any vacation time or sick leave stocked up that you could use?"

"Yes," she answered slowly. It wasn't that she was afraid to answer . . . but she was wary. Very wary.

"And can you use it anytime you want?"

"Yes. At least for the next month or two." A frown puckered her forehead and her glasses slipped a fraction.

"I was just thinking you might like to spend some time with Cappy, get to know her before any, uh, decisions are made."

"Of course, I'd like that. As a matter of fact, I was going to ask you about spending time with Caroline before I . . . before we even think of any changes." The tension eased. "I was hoping I could have her for an afternoon or a day here and there. We really do need the chance to get to know each other." She'd been very much mistaken. This was going to work out almost exactly as she'd planned. She knew she needed some breaking-in time with her niece and here he was offering it up to her on a platter.

Mac stretched out his legs, tipped back his cap, and knew, without a shadow of a doubt, that what he was about to suggest would send her into a tailspin. A tailspin, if he was guessing correctly, she'd try furiously to cover. "You could really help me out, Elizabeth. I'm going on a fishing trip for a couple of weeks with a buddy of mine, and my sister Kate had volunteered to keep Cappy. But if you're free, that would be even better. Seeing as how you're so anxious to spend time with her."

She was very careful to keep even a hint of self-satisfaction off her face and out of her voice. This was perfect. She'd be able to take her niece, get her settled in, arrange for a nanny, adjust her daily routine—in short, have things running so smoothly that by the time he returned he'd hardly be able to argue about which environment was better for Caroline. "I'd be happy to help you out, Mac. Do you have a particular date in mind?"

"Yep. I'll be leaving a week from Monday. Could you move in then?"

This time, she almost dropped the glass. "Move in? I'm afraid I don't understand."

"Well now, Elizabeth, it's real simple. You have time off; I need a baby-sitter. You bring a suitcase; I provide a bed."

She felt conned and not a little miffed by that drawling, down-home speech of his. "I'm afraid we have a bit of misunderstanding, Mac. I'd be delighted to have Caroline—but naturally I'd prefer to have her in my own home."

"Sure, I understand that, but we're talking about Cappy. We're talking about what's best for her, aren't we? Well, Elizabeth, I just guarantee you we should go really easy on the changes with that little tyke. She's had a bunch already."

She'd been outwitted, outmaneuvered, by a man she'd completely underestimated, and there wasn't any way now she could insist she take Caroline to her home and not appear heartless and unfeeling. It almost hurt her to smile but she did. "You've made a very good point, Mac. I certainly don't want to upset Caroline. If you think it's better for me to stay with her at your house, then I'll be there."

"That's great, Elizabeth. I appreciate it." It didn't really seem all that great to him, but he'd give her a chance with the pipsqueak— and just to make sure she didn't goof it up completely, he'd alert Kate and Mandy. He reached for his baseball cap, shoved it on, and stood. Two weeks of diapers and dribble would probably be all the lady would need to let this sudden maternal urge of hers die a natural death. "I'd better get going. I have a couple of things I need to do."

She was so glad he was leaving, she practically catapulted from the chair. "I'll see you a week from Monday, then." She stretched out her hand. "I'll call in a couple of days so we can get organized."

He took her hand in his and grinned. He had to give it to her. She had a lot of guts jumping in like this—especially since he knew she didn't know beans about babies. Her handshake was firm and brisk—as he'd known it would be—but she was pushing away at those glasses of hers again. He'd bet it was a nervous habit that she'd had a long time and he'd also be willing to bet she wasn't the least aware of it. It told him a little more about Elizabeth. She wasn't quite as cool and calm as she wanted folks to believe. If and when he got to know her better, he'd let her know it made her just a tad more likable.

Elizabeth stood at the doorway and watched Mac stride down the hall. She felt stunned. Had she really just agreed to stay at that man's house for two whole weeks? She flexed her fingers slowly as she stepped back into the room. She could still feel the pressure of his hand on hers. It was a callused, rough-skinned hand, yet so very, very gentle. The thought rose like a bubble to the surface of a pond. Hadn't she watched that hand cradle a baby and stroke a dog? She nearly snorted out loud in disbelief as she swung the door shut. What in the world was happening to her? The man meant nothing to her. Caroline was her sole concern. She crossed the room and picked up the photograph of her niece and pressed it against her chest.

Chapter Three

Elizabeth stopped her car at the curb in front of Mac's house at exactly two minutes before eight on Monday morning. Her fear was as pure as Ivory soap and just short of paralyzing. Her hands, clutched tight on the steering wheel, were icy, her brain foggy, and her heart despairing. How in the world had she, a seemingly intelligent, sensible woman, ever imagined she could take care of an infant for fourteen whole days? Alone. With absolutely no experience.

Twenty-four hours after that awful, awkward meeting with Mac, the enormity of her decision to baby-sit had sunk in. It had sent her in a panic to the bookstore. She'd bought Dr. Spock, five other books by more current gurus on child care, and every magazine she could find on infants. She'd called three day-care centers to ask if she could come and watch them with the babies. They'd thought her request odd, perhaps suspicious. Abandoning that idea, she'd rooted through her Rolodex searching for a friend with a baby and found an acquaintance with a three-year-old. She'd promptly invited the whole family for a visit. It hadn't taken five minutes to realize a three-year-old was not quite the same thing as a six-month-old. And it had taken two hours to put her house back together.

Slowly, she pulled her hands from the steering wheel and turned off the ignition. None of the reading and talking had helped. Nor had she gotten any vote of confidence from her secretary, Peggy. Quite the opposite, in fact. As she recalled their conversation yesterday, Peggy had told her, tongue planted firmly in cheek, that she would be saying loads of prayers to St. Jude—a special saint invoked for hopeless cases.

Her stomach was in knots as she got out of the car. Heat shimmered off the black asphalt. The humid, hot air was as smothering as a cloying perfume. It was much too late to wish she'd leveled with Mac and told him she'd never taken care of a baby—or any child, for that matter. She hauled two of her suitcases from the backseat and staggered toward the

front porch. The blinding white glare of the sun
made her stumble and trip on the first step. One
small thought kept her from turning back and
running for her life. Every year, thousands of
women became brand spanking new mothers
with no more experience than she and somehow . . . somehow they managed.

When Mac swung open the front door, it
suddenly occurred to Elizabeth that there was
one slight difference between herself and those
thousands of women having their very first babies. She had no husband to count on for sup-
port. Sucking in a ragged breath, she lifted her
chin, looked Mac smack in the eye, and forced
herself to smile. If this man could learn to be
a mom of sorts, then so could she!

He liked her in jeans, Mac thought as he
shouldered open the screen door and took the
suitcases from her over her expected objection.
Even the fancy designer kind she was wearing.
He noticed her cream-colored blouse next. He
guessed it was silk—not a smart choice. If she
was going to wear that sort of thing while taking care of Cappy, her dry-cleaning bills were
going to be astronomical.

When he introduced her to Jake, his fishing
buddy and assistant coach, he couldn't keep the
grin off his face. Jake practically stammered
when he said hello—and shot Mac a look that
said, *Why didn't you tell me she was such a*

looker? Elizabeth didn't seem to notice. Not that Mac thought she would.

She was all business, as usual, and bustled into the house as if on a mission. Mac could almost feel the temperature in the room dropping. He wondered how long it would take Jake to feel the chill.

Elizabeth nearly fell over all the gear piled willy-nilly around the room. There were fishing poles, backpacks, sleeping bags, and ice chests, all of it competing for space with the same clutter of baby equipment she'd seen before. The Beach Boys were singing about California girls at earsplitting decibels, a fine layer of dust covered the furniture, and Caroline sat dozing in her swing as it rocked to and fro. The dog was flopped down right next to the baby and Elizabeth froze when she spotted it.

Lazily, Colleen opened one eye and looked her over. Elizabeth felt her adrenaline surge and took a step backward. Mac caught her by the shoulders.

"It's okay, Elizabeth. You just took Coll by surprise the last time." She was somewhat reassured when the dog's tail swished slowly across the floor.

She knew there was no point in arguing with Mac about the dog. Again. She'd tried to convince him to take the animal to one of his sisters or even a kennel. He'd flatly refused, on the grounds that Colleen was an excellent

watchdog and he wanted to leave town knowing she and Cappy were protected.

His hands on her shoulders were disconcert-
ing. Elizabeth could feel the heat—and the
comfort. Pulling away, she took a small note-
book from her purse and flipped it open.

''I know you want to get going as soon as
you can, so I just jotted down a few questions
I needed to ask you.''

Mac rolled his eyes at Jake, who still had
the look of a love-struck pup plastered all over
his face. More questions? He'd already answered hundreds of them for her every time
she'd called him. And he'd long since lost
track of the number of times she'd phoned. At
her insistence, he'd written out a list of instruc-
tions for her as long as his arm. He should have
known that wouldn't be enough for this lady.

He sucked in a breath and caught a whiff of
her perfume. It was light, exotic, and he
guessed it was something expensive. Her head
was bent and in profile and the band of sun
streaming in the window turned her hair to fire
and her skin translucent. He felt an inexplica-
ble urge to smooth back the ringlets that fell
against the curve of her cheek and tell her to
calm down, take it easy. And then she went
and shoved those glasses back on and frowned
like some grim, disapproving schoolmarm and
he sighed and crooked his finger. ''Come on,
Elizabeth, I'll show you where all the stuff is

that you'll need, while you ask me your questions.''

Forty-five minutes later, he and Jake finally began to load their gear in Jake's Bronco. He had Elizabeth sitting on the porch swing with the baby in her lap and the dog at her feet. She wasn't looking very comfortable and she was still managing to fire questions at him every time he came up the porch steps. He hoped that by nightfall she'd calm down enough to get Cappy to bed. But he had Kate checking in with her that evening just to make sure.

''You girls have a good time.'' Mac bent over and bussed Cappy soundly. ''If you need me, Elizabeth, just call the number I left by the phone. That's Sheriff Jacobsen's office. He'll know where to find me.''

''We'll be just fine, Mac.'' Elizabeth hoped she sounded matter-of-fact, in control. ''And good luck with the fishing.''

''Hope you have a big freezer, Elizabeth.'' Jake ambled up the steps. He was still grinning ear to ear. Mac figured the guy was immune to drops in temperature. ''We'll bring you a mess of 'em.''

''Why, thank you, Jake,'' she replied faintly. She was afraid to ask if she'd be expected to clean them.

''Take care, now.'' Mac gave her a brief salute with Jake still hanging at his shoulder. ''Thanks for helping me out.''

Elizabeth nodded and made herself smile brightly. "You're very welcome. And don't you worry about us. We're going to get along famously."

Her smile died the second Mac turned his back and loped down the stairs.

The Bronco roared off, leaving a silence that was filled only by the sounds of birds tittering high in the trees, the squeak of the porch swing—and her own thumping heartbeat. The baby stirred in her lap and she swallowed—hard.

"We'll be just fine," she whispered fiercely. They just had to be. She tightened her arms around the baby's tummy and Caroline cooed. Elizabeth knew she couldn't ever begin to describe the feeling it gave her.

An hour later, she was testing the baby formula on her wrist like Mac had shown her. It was much too hot. The baby was fussy and her whimpers were getting stronger and louder by the second.

"It's coming, Caroline. Won't be a minute." She tried to keep the panic out of her voice. How was she to cool the bottle down? Run it under cold water? Stick it in a bowl of ice cubes? She opened the freezer and stopped. The solution was simple. Simply stick it in the freezer for a minute. She turned back to her niece. Caroline's eyes squeezed shut and two large teardrops rolled down her cheeks.

"Oh, sweetie, please don't cry." Elizabeth picked her up from the infant seat and slid one arm under her bottom. Caroline stopped crying and stared at Elizabeth, eyes round and wide.

"Oh, dear. You're wet." The baby drooled and stuffed her fist into her mouth.

"Right. You need to be changed. No problem." The silk blouse had been a bad choice, she now realized. "There's absolutely nothing to changing a diaper." She felt a tad silly talking to someone who couldn't answer back, but it seemed to be a morale booster—and she needed that. She laid Caroline on the changing table and reached for the snap on the leg of her playsuit. The baby chortled and stuck her feet straight up in the air.

"Hold on a minute, sweetie." The fabric slipped from her fingers as Caroline began working her legs like pistons.

A half hour later, Elizabeth gathered her niece in her arms and groaned. This changing business was nothing less than an ordeal. The playsuit wasn't snapped closed but the diaper was finally changed and that seemed a minor miracle. Wearily, she walked down the hall as Caroline squirmed and began to make small, unhappy, and undoubtedly hungry noises.

"Oh, no." She stopped at the kitchen door and stared at the fridge. The bottle! It was in the freezer. Bracing the baby awkwardly against her hip (Mac had made it look so easy), she flung open the freezer door and grabbed the bottle. It was as frosted as the trays of ice that sat on the shelf. Caroline's voice raised a couple of decibels and Elizabeth jiggled her inexpertly as she stuck the bottle in the microwave.

"Just one little minute, honey." She felt as unhappy as the baby. When the timer went off, she was near tears herself. Plunked down on a hard-backed chair, she stuck the bottle in Caroline's mouth. For a full minute, she kept waiting for something to happen. She didn't know what exactly; she was simply anticipating the worst. Five minutes later, she let herself relax. The silence, broken only by the contented sucking of her niece, was sheer bliss.

When the doorbell rang at eight o'clock that night, Elizabeth was flopped on the couch, completely exhausted. She hadn't yet mastered the art of diapering, Caroline hadn't napped longer than a minute or two all day, and she was sure the baby hadn't gotten a fourth of the baby food she'd fixed her into her mouth. But her niece had finally drunk several ounces of formula and had fallen asleep in her arms. Elizabeth had put her to bed, fed Colleen, who treated her like her best friend when she doled out her food, and then collapsed. She hadn't yet figured out what to do with Caroline other than hold her. And her blouse was a mess.

Rising wearily, she went to the door with the dog at her heels.

The family resemblance was incredible, Elizabeth thought as she ushered the woman into the house.

"Hi! You must be Elizabeth. I'm Kate, Mac's sister." She was nearly as tall as her brother and when she smiled, it was uncanny, for it was Mac's smile—wide, open, and embracing. "I just thought I'd pop over and see how you were getting along. I hope you don't mind?"

"Oh, no. Not at all." Part of her wondered if Mac had asked Kate to come and see if she and Caroline were still breathing—and part of her was simply very glad to see another adult human being. "Come in. May I get you a cup of coffee or a soda?"

Kate laughed. "A Coke would be great. But I can get it."

"No, please sit down. I'll just be a minute."

"You've talked me into it. I'm pooped, I can tell you."

Elizabeth went to the kitchen with Colleen close behind. The dog still made her uneasy but feeding her had apparently cemented a bond of some sort—at least from the dog's point of view. The dog's tail thumped against her leg as she opened the fridge and she reached back and stroked her head. There was a certain satisfaction in having made a friend of the beast. She wasn't sure that would apply to her niece and for certain it didn't apply to the uncle. All in all, she thought as she collected glasses and napkins, Colleen had given her sagging confidence a much-needed lift.

As she returned to the living room, she racked her brain trying to recall how many children Mac had told her Kate had.

Kate solved that problem as she took the glass of Coke Elizabeth handed her. "Ah, that looks lovely. Four of my five little darlings have been sick for a week and Jerry was out of town. He got back an hour ago, took one look at me, and said I needed to get out of the house for a while. So I hope you don't mind my just barging in like this."

"Heavens no. I'm glad you stopped by. Are your children better? Was it something serious?" Five children, four sick? The thought of it made her feel faint. Yet Kate was smiling and didn't look terribly distraught.

"Oh, no. Just a stomach flu one of the older ones brought home from day camp. Naturally, it spread like wildfire. But with my group, it usually does. Don't mind me," Kate added cheerfully. "I may gripe a lot, but I wouldn't know what to do without them."

"Of course you wouldn't." Elizabeth smiled wanly. Stomach flu? The images that conjured up made her determined not to let her niece anywhere near her cousins. The thought of

Caroline even having a sniffle scared her to death.

Kate raised her glass. ''I want you to know, Elizabeth, that we all think it was so good of you to come here and stay with Caroline. I'd have taken her, but Mac said you were very anxious to spend some time with her.''

Elizabeth breathed a sigh of relief. Apparently Mac hadn't told Kate she wanted custody of Caroline. And she certainly didn't want to be the one to tell her. ''I was glad to help out.''

''Well, as far as I'm concerned, the more family the better.'' Kate smiled, then breezily changed the subject, which reassured Elizabeth, yet filled her with guilt. Kate was so friendly—but how friendly would she be if she knew Elizabeth wanted to take her niece away from their family?

An hour later, Kate left. She'd spent the time regaling Elizabeth with stories of Mike and Eileen, Caroline's parents, and how happy they'd been together and how pleased she'd been when her sister and her husband had decided to live close by. She'd confided that Eileen and Michael had considered Caroline a miracle because they'd tried for some years to have a baby.

She spoke of the accident briefly, but didn't hesitate to talk about the grief and the loss that they all still felt.

And then she'd talked about Mac and his short-lived professional football career. She explained how he'd fractured his tibia twice, once in college, the second time during his first season in the pros. The doctors had warned him that one more break could leave him limping for life. He'd decided to quit but couldn't leave the game entirely. When the high school had offered him the job of coaching, he'd jumped at it. He was, Kate had proudly assured her, the best coach the school had ever had.

To Elizabeth's relief, Kate hadn't tried to pry into her past or ask why she hadn't tried to contact her half-brother until recently. She'd only said, in that warm way of hers, how very glad she was to welcome Elizabeth into the family.

Elizabeth felt she almost understood, as she waved good-bye from the porch, why Michael had come to live in this small town. Maybe she even envied him.

She slept in the rocking chair in Caroline's room that night, afraid that if she slept in Mac's room she might not hear the baby if she awakened.

In the morning she changed her mind. She was stiff and sore and there wasn't a way in the world she wouldn't hear Caroline. Her niece was hollering loud enough to be heard blocks away. She squinted at the clock and groaned. Five A.M.?

"Caroline," she said as she lifted the baby carefully from the crib, "this is not a civilized hour to be getting up."

Her niece squealed with delight and grabbed a fistful of Elizabeth's hair.

It took her several fairly painful minutes to release the baby's tight grip on her hair. But she forgot her tender scalp a second later.

Caroline smiled and said something that sounded to Elizabeth like "ma-ma". The feeling it gave her made her weak in the knees.

The diapering was still difficult though, and breakfast a mess, but she'd done it. She'd made it through the first twenty-four hours! She knew Mac hadn't thought she'd make it one minute.

By eight o'clock that night, Caroline was asleep and Elizabeth could hardly keep her eyes open. Her plan to start cleaning the house was dimming fast. Not that it didn't need it. And the yard didn't bear thinking about. The grass was mowed, but the weeds had taken over every inch of garden space. She stifled a yawn. Tomorrow. When Caroline was napping—*if* she would nap. Today hadn't been too successful in that regard.

She hesitated at the door to Mac's bedroom. Exhaustion won. Climbing into his bed, she pulled the quilt up to her chin and closed her eyes. Seconds later, they flew open. She closed her eyes firmly again—and still saw him in her mind. Saw the way the tiny lines at the corners of his eyes crinkled when he smiled and the way his wide, mobile mouth curved, and she could almost hear the low rumble, deep in his chest, when he laughed.

She turned over on her side irritably. What *was* the matter with her? The man was Caroline's uncle. Period. As she drifted into sleep, she could almost feel, again, the pressure of his hands on her shoulders. And she liked it—she liked the remembering.

Mac stood in the doorway to his bedroom and looked down at Elizabeth. Her arm was flung out of the covers and her hair was spread over the pillow. Moonlight colored her in grays and silvers and he could see the quilt flutter with every breath she took. She looked very feminine and very touchable. His lips curved. He figured he wouldn't get many chances to see her this way.

He moved a little closer to the bed and decided he wasn't entirely unhappy the fishing trip had come to such an abrupt end—though Jake wouldn't like the cast on his arm or the one encasing his knee.

What had amazed him, once he'd left, was that he'd thought about her. He'd wondered how she was faring with the baby and the dog and wondered why he'd had to convince himself that he didn't really need to call her the first night he was away.

It was unnecessary, now. With Jake laid up, there'd be no more fishing for a while. The middle of July was a lousy time, anyway. Next summer they'd go no later than June—if he could find someone to coach the girls' softball team.

The problem now was sleep. It was four A.M. He'd stayed at the hospital with Jake until he was sure everything was going all right— and then he'd come home. And she was in his bed.

He'd told her to sleep there. But it didn't leave him many choices, other than a couch or two. Quietly, he left the room and went to Cappy's door. The baby was sleeping as soundly as Elizabeth. Padding down the hall, he grabbed sheets and a blanket from the linen closet and headed for the den. He thought about a shower and dismissed it. The plumbing, old and noisy, wouldn't wake Cappy, but it might wake Elizabeth. Unbuttoning his shirt, he thanked the dog, who sauntered in for some attention, for not barking. He put on some sweatpants from his backpack, tossed his clothes on the chair, kicked the dog out, and closed the door. His last thought was of Elizabeth, hair fanned across the pillow, her arm curled up close to her cheek, looking vulnerable as hell.

*   *   *

Elizabeth came awake slowly. She heard a funny sound, a gurgling sort of sound. Her eyes opened wide. A cooing sound. Caroline! She leaped from the bed and ran down the hall.

The baby was kicking again, wildly, and making happy noises. She halted at the doorway. It was the mobile. Her niece stared at it with delight, and with every movement she made, the mobile responded. Elizabeth backed out quietly into the hall. Maybe this morning she'd have time to brush her teeth and make some coffee.

She'd never moved so fast. She ran to the kitchen, got the coffee going, and dashed to the bathroom. Teeth brushed and face washed, she headed back to Caroline's room and stopped cold. The dog was standing by the door to the den.

Oh, no! The hair on the nape of her neck rose and she clapped a hand to her mouth. The door had been wide open last night. She'd swear to it. And now it was closed.

She fought the sudden and unexpected fear that welled up in her throat. Could someone be in there? Should she go get the baby and run for it? Or call the police and then run? She wasn't sure. Indecision threatened to paralyze her. Colleen stood stiffly by the door, huge and menacing. Could she count on her to scare away an intruder—*if* there was an intruder?

She wasn't certain, especially since the animal was wagging her tail. Creeping forward, she felt the goose bumps prickling her skin as she tiptoed to the door. *Stay calm. Don't panic, Elizabeth,* she told herself sternly.

She listened for a moment, ear pressed to the door, her heart a suffocating lump in her throat. There was nothing. No sounds, no hints of stealthy movements. Maybe the door had simply closed shut by itself. Reason told her that was unlikely. She clutched frantically at the dog's collar and Colleen began to whine. ''Hush,'' she whispered.

The baby was starting to make loud, unhappy sounds. It was now or never. Summoning up what few shreds of courage she had at her command and her largely untested hope in the size, if not the courage, of Colleen, she pushed open the door and screamed, ''Get him.''

The noises woke Mac. A gentle bump against the door, a whine, someone whispering. And from farther away, Cappy. Her voice was revving up. Cappy! What the heck had happened? And Elizabeth! He bolted from the couch and reached for the door. It caught him in the face with a thunk.

Staggering back, he was enveloped in a blur of arms, legs, and fur. The dog snarled, Elizabeth screamed, and Mac grunted as his body collided with the two of them. In the background he could hear the wailing cries of a very unhappy baby.

Mac found himself, after the dog was untangled and had slunk out, with an armful of Elizabeth—a yelling, pummeling Elizabeth, smelling of toothpaste and soap.

"Hold on, now! Take it easy. It's Mac. It's just me."

"Oh, thank goodness. It's you!" For a moment, Elizabeth went all soft and yielding in his arms. And then she went all stiff and rigid. "It's *you!*"

"You're right. Only me."

"Do you have any idea how you scared me? And you've scared Caroline—and even Colleen!" She gulped in a mouthful of air. "How could you do such a thing!"

"I wish I knew." He had to swallow his chuckle. Cappy was just hollering to be fed and Coll was totally confused. Only Elizabeth was scared silly. And how could he help but enjoy her like this? All fury and female curves—in all the right places. It wouldn't last long, he knew that. But she'd stopped flailing around, and now she felt soft and warm and clinging in his arms. He knew he shouldn't enjoy this, if he knew what was good for him. He wasn't prepared for her kind of trouble—nor, he suspected, was she.

Elizabeth wasn't sure she heard him at all, for what she became acutely aware of was the way she had her arms wrapped tightly around his neck. His arms were around her too, resting low on her back, pulling her up against him. She could feel the pressure of each of his fingers splayed around her waist, feel the crush of his rock-solid chest.

She jerked away and stared at him. He was standing there in his sweatpants with no shirt. ''You're not dressed!''

''I'm usually not when I'm sleeping.'' He grinned and lowered his eyes, taking in the pristine white nightgown, edged in lace, that hung gracefully past her knees.

She'd completely forgotten. No robe. Just a cotton nightgown. She scuttled backward out the door.

''You go get something on while I get Cappy. Okay?'' Mac said gently.

She heard him chuckling as she ran for his bedroom. And felt herself blushing. Darn him!

When he picked up Cappy, he very promptly held her out at arm's length. She was dripping like a faucet. It was hard to screw up a disposable diaper but he saw what Elizabeth had done when he peeled the sleeper off. The tape was too low and close to the edge and Cappy's kicking had pulled it loose. She was going to need a bath bright and early this morning. He stripped her down to her rosy pink skin and took her straight to the tub.

Elizabeth stayed out of the way while Mac was bathing Caroline. She didn't want to tell him she'd only sponged her off yesterday. The idea of handling a soapy, wet baby had been frightening. She'd pictured drownings—or worse.

She used the time to take a lightning-fast shower, towel dry her hair, and throw on a pair of shorts and an oversized cotton blouse. And tried to get rid of the image of a bare-chested Mac with a two-day growth of beard and sleep-mussed hair—and the feel of his arms around her.

Chapter Four

Twenty-five minutes later, Elizabeth had finished giving Caroline her bottle and was waiting for Mac to get out of the shower. The baby was in the swing and Elizabeth was pacing the room, her thoughts jumbled. Once again, there'd been an unfortunate scene. And once again, she'd ended up looking foolish, nearly hysterical. She wasn't sure just what it was about Mac, but it was beginning to seem inevitable that some disaster would occur whenever she was around him. But how, she thought irritably, was she to have known he was in the house? More to the point, why was he back again just two days after he'd left?

Distracted, she ran her finger through a film of dust on the end table. Was it possible Kate had called him? No, she decided, not possible. Kate hadn't a devious bone in her body and she would surely have told her if she'd planned to call Mac.

"Hello, sweetheart."

Elizabeth spun around at the sound of Mac's voice and saw him, mug in hand, bending over the swing. His hair was wet, his clothing clean but disreputable.

"How's my girl?"

Caroline was smiling and Mac was smiling and Elizabeth stood stock-still and tried to identify the feeling that gripped her. The baby's tiny fingers closed around one of Mac's and she was blowing bubbles that brought a delighted chuckle from him. Just as Mac turned toward her, Elizabeth knew how she felt. Closed out. Alone. It was the two of them. And her.

The unexpected tears in her eyes shocked her, but no more so than the mental image that rose, seemingly out of nowhere. She saw clearly, yet for no longer than a fraction of a moment, a young girl, her tear-stained face pressed against a window. Alone. Her hands balled into fists and she blinked hard, willing away the tears that threatened and the unwanted image.

"Good morning, again." Mac gave Elizabeth a lopsided grin as he took a slurp of the steaming-hot coffee.

From this distance and without her glasses, Mac and Caroline were a bit blurred—as was the state of her emotions. Both of them came into focus when she stuck her glasses back on. She shoved her hands into her pockets and her emotions deep inside.

"Good morning, Mac."

My goodness. Mac scratched his head thoughtfully. Only Elizabeth could say good morning and make it sound like some sort of formal pronouncement. That haughty voice and the way she was standing, poker straight, stiff and wary as a spooked animal, was his warning: a red flag that let him know something was definitely troubling the lady. He'd lay odds it had something to do with him showing up in the wee hours of the morning. He'd go easy and let her tell him—as he knew she would.

"Sorry I scared you this morning, Elizabeth."

"I wouldn't say you scared me, actually." Elizabeth's jaw raised a fraction. "I was simply concerned . . . for the baby."

He wanted to chuckle, but didn't. And he wouldn't remind her she'd actually said she was scared. Matter of fact, he'd been a little scared himself when she and Coll had stormed into the room. But she seemed to need some face-saving and he was willing to give it to her. "Sure, I understand."

Elizabeth sat down very carefully on the edge of a chair on the far side of the room and tried to ignore the niggling suspicion that Mac's "understanding" had more to do with pity. She certainly didn't want his pity and she didn't know why she was bothering to explain her behavior this morning, anyway. The very first priority was to find out why he'd returned so unexpectedly. "I'm assuming you have some sort of explanation for your, uh, middle-of-the-night arrival?"

Mac hunkered down and gave Cappy's swing another windup, buying himself a little time. He needed to get the smile off his face. She had such a prissy way of talking. It could've been really annoying except he'd finally figured out it was her way of covering up when she was feeling uncomfortable.

"Well, now, Elizabeth," he said as kindly as he could, "Jake took a bad fall last night and broke a couple of bones. We didn't get to the hospital until about one A.M. and it was after four when I got home. I just didn't see any sense in waking you up."

So Mac hadn't come back to check on her after all! Her cheeks grew hot and her eyes skittered away from his. Well, that was what happened when you made assumptions without knowing the facts, she chided herself. She was certainly sorry to hear about Jake's injuries and she felt just a little sorry for herself—and sorry about the not-so-kind thoughts she'd harbored about Mac and his motives. "Oh, Mac. I'm sorry to hear about Jake. How did it happen?"

"A late-night nature call without a flashlight." The look on her face told him she didn't have a clue. "The bathroom, Elizabeth. He was on his way to the bathroom and he tripped and fell in the dark."

"Oh." Elizabeth shook her head slightly. Would this propensity of hers to appear completely ignorant in front of this man ever stop? She shifted the conversation—such as it was—back to Jake. "Is he going to be all right?"

"He's going to be fine, though he won't like having to hobble around for a couple of months." He'd watched the color rise in her cheeks and knew she was embarrassed for having thought he'd snuck home to see how she was faring with his sweetie. His mug of coffee was still half full, but he thought she could use a break. "I need more coffee. Can I get you some?"

"No, thank you." It was slowly dawning on her that her troubles were just beginning. What was she to do now that Mac was home?

"Be right back." Mac saw her frown and fiddle with her glasses and he knew what was coming. Questions. Lots of questions. It was enough to make a strong man feel faint. Entering the kitchen, he checked the clock on the stove. He'd give her no more than three minutes before she'd come bustling in.

It took her only one.

"Mac, I think, in light of these, uh, unexpected developments, we need to discuss our situation."

He leaned against the kitchen counter and kept his face as blank as a new sheet of paper. She couldn't just say something simple like, "I need to talk to you." Nope. Not her. His mouth twitched. It seemed to him that Ms. Kincaid sure could use a few lessons on how to lighten up and relax. He set his mug on the counter and grinned. She didn't know it, but the school bell just rang. "Let's go to the park."

"I beg your pardon?" Elizabeth stared at him over the rim of her glasses as if he'd spoken in tongues.

"The park. You know—green grass, picnic tables, swings."

"I know what a park is," she snapped. It was simple. She absolutely could not understand this man. She'd never understand him. And apparently he'd missed the point. Or never got it in the first place. "What I'm trying to tell you, Mac, is that we need to rethink our arrangements."

Mercy, mercy. Some people couldn't walk and chew gum at the same time. Mac hitched his thumbs in his pockets. "You want us to have a talk, right? I agree. We need to, but as far as I know, there's no law that says we can't do our talking anywhere we want.''

''What about Caroline?''

''Shoot, Elizabeth, fresh air and sunshine are good for babies.''

Elizabeth winced. Mac had suggested before his trip that she take Caroline outside and she hadn't. She'd thought it too hot, there were too many insects, and, in truth, she'd been too nervous.

Mac's voice became gentle as he watched her fool with her glasses again. There was a worried little frown right between her eyebrows, her hair was still damp and curling all over the place, and he needed to get the heck out of the kitchen before he succumbed to the urge to tangle his fingers in those thick, riotous tresses. ''Look, why don't you grab some tennis shoes and we'll get going, okay?''

Elizabeth wiggled her toes in the bit of leather that passed for sandals. He was making this sound more like a hike than a stroll but she really couldn't think of a reason to object so she simply nodded and hurried from the room.

''What's one more bit of craziness, anyway?'' she mumbled to herself as she rummaged in the pocket of her suitcase. Pulling out a pair of Reeboks, she laced them up quickly.

So they'd go to the park.

The breakfast dishes weren't done, the bed wasn't made, and they had decisions to make.

But they'd go to the park.

She fumbled in her pocket, searching for her watch, and came up empty. She scanned the room—bedside table, dresser—and saw it lying on the top of the bureau. For the life of her she couldn't remember putting it there last night, though when she thought about it, she'd hardly been in a condition to remember much, given the state of exhaustion she'd been in. Picking up the watch, she glanced at the framed photographs clustered at the back of the bureau. There were pictures of Mac's parents, his sisters and their children, Eileen and Michael with Caroline, and pictures of Mac with all of them. One more photo caught her eye as she leaned closer. It was of Mac and a woman. A pretty woman with hair the color of buttercups. Mac had his arms around her waist and her arms were around his neck. Their position was much the way she had found herself with Mac this morning.

Of course, that unplanned embrace had been a mistake, an unfortunate accident. Not like this photograph of Mac and the yellow-haired woman, purposefully holding on to each other.

A hunk. That would be the word her secretary would use to describe Mac. She was sure of it. Her shoelace was too loose and she bent down to retie it. Even in the ragged cutoffs and faded T-shirt he was decked out in today, he still fit the requisite criteria needed for *that* one-word description. She marched through the house to the front door, thinking how absolutely grateful she was that the men in her life brought other adjectives to mind.

Mac was waiting out on the sidewalk, rocking Caroline in the carriage, and Elizabeth felt a sharp twinge of guilt over her none-too-charitable assessment of him. He was, of course, she told herself, an obviously caring uncle, completely devoted to his niece. But it was also very clear that he had little ambition and the drive to succeed she admired in the men she knew.

"Are you sure it isn't too hot in here for Caroline?" Elizabeth bent over the carriage parked by the picnic table and touched her niece's cheek. It had to be pushing ninety and it wasn't ten o'clock in the morning.

"Nope. But we're not going to be keeping her in there, anyway." Mac released the dog from her leash then reached over the buggy handle and picked up Cappy. "Okay, pumpkin, let's go."

Elizabeth looked at him quizzically. "Go? Where are we going?" She'd just assumed they'd sit here at the table shaded by a stand of leafy trees.

"Not far." Mac shifted the baby into the crook of his arm and grabbed her by the elbow. The dog took off at a run. Elizabeth wasn't that willing. He could tell she was hanging back, dragging her feet. Worried, as usual.

She stumbled when Mac's hand moved down her arm and grasped hers. Nerve endings tingled and heated under the slide of his palm over her skin. His fingers laced through hers, curling possessively. His thumb pressed against her wrist where her pulse had begun to race. Her fingers were equally responsive until her brain got a second message and she let her hand go limp in his.

She saw his lips curve as he gently pulled her forward, giving her no choice but to move with him or dig in stubbornly and cause a scene. And he didn't seem to think it odd that he should be hauling her across the field, hand in hand, like old friends—or more than friends. Annoyed, she let him pull her along across the open grassy area and tried to ignore the rub of his callused palm on hers and the feel of the sun-bleached hair on his arm tickling lightly against her wrist. All sensation was forgotten when he stopped directly in front of the playground equipment.

"So what do you want to do first? Swing or slide?"

"I beg your pardon?" Pulling her hand free, Elizabeth jerked around and looked Mac right in the eye. She didn't know what she expected to see on his face, some crazed or half-demented expression maybe. But he couldn't have looked saner—except his mouth was twitching and his gray eyes were twinkling with undisguised mischief.

"Oh, I get it. You can't decide. Well then, let's swing first." He hooked the swing toward her. "Hop on. I'll give you a push."

"Good heavens, Mac." She laughed nervously and looked around. Luckily there wasn't another soul in sight. "I don't swing."

"Never? Not even as a kid?"

"Well, yes. Of course. I suppose everyone did."

"Good. I won't have to teach you, then." Without so much as a please or a thank you, he maneuvered her around so her back was to the swing.

Obviously, the man had no shame. And she couldn't refuse. Not with that sniggering, gotcha-look on his face and the round-eyed stare of her niece. Furious with the two of them, she let herself be lowered onto a seat that wasn't a real seat at all, just a broad band of hot, black rubber. Her glasses slipped down her nose a fraction and, impatiently, she pushed them back up.

Mac plucked them off.

"You don't want them to fall off and break," he said. Folding them up, he stuck them in his T-shirt pocket. ''Hang on! Here you go.''

She barely had time to clutch the chains before she began to move. Mac's hand smacked at her back. The chains squeaked, and with each firm push that he gave her, she flew higher and higher. Without thinking, she lifted her legs, sticking them straight out in front of her so they wouldn't touch the ground. It was so instinctive, she nearly giggled. There were some things you never forgot and swinging was apparently one of them. Her breath caught in her throat as the swing rocked skyward. The hot, steamy air ruffled her hair, ballooned her blouse, caressed her skin. She felt like the wind, like a bird.

It was ridiculous.

It was exhilarating.

She was mortified.

She was loving it.

Her hands gripped the chains so tight, it almost hurt. But not enough to intrude on the moment, on the magic Mac was creating for her. She was riding high, relishing the sweet summer smells of honeysuckle and new-mown grass. Mac's hand slapped at her back again, sending a tingle that went straight down her spine. A snippet of a poem, long forgotten, came back to her.

> *''Up in the air and over the wall,*
> *Till I can see so wide. . . . ''*

She twisted around and looked back at Mac and Caroline. The baby's smile was ear to ear. Mac winked and gave her a thumbs-up, as if she were accomplishing some stupendous feat. She felt her chest swell with an absurd pride— as if she actually believed she'd done something wonderful. She forgot to keep her legs up and her shoes scraped the ground, spraying dirt to her knees and bumping her to a jerky stop.

''Had enough?'' Mac didn't wait for her answer. He figured she had and there wasn't any sense in pushing things too far. ''Okay. It's our turn.'' Mac settled into the swing with one arm encircling Cappy and the other holding on to the chain. ''Give us a good shove.''

When Elizabeth gave him a push, she heard the baby shriek with delight. Her lips parted and she chuckled. This was the silliest thing she'd ever done—and she was loving every minute of it. Her hands touched again on Mac's broad back as he urged her to push harder and she felt his muscles ripple beneath the warm, cotton fabric.

Over and over again she reached out and pushed. The wind ruffled Mac's already unruly hair as he bent his head to the baby he held in his arms. It wasn't so wide a world, she thought. Just a bit of a playground with a man in a faded gray shirt and a baby in pink with hair the color of carrots.

Two little boys came running toward the swings, their mother not far behind them. Thoroughly embarrassed, Elizabeth dropped her arms to her sides and backed away.

He'd forget the slide, Mac decided. Elizabeth's face was about the same color as Cappy's hair—and it wasn't from sunburn. She'd had enough for now. But it was a good beginning. She'd actually loosened up and laughed, if only for a few minutes. He whistled for Colleen, who was enjoying the attention the two boys were giving her. Elizabeth nearly sprinted back to the picnic table. He ambled behind with the baby and wondered what he was doing trying to entertain a lady who rubbed him the wrong way every time she opened her mouth. And why.

Mac propped his elbows on the rough redwood table and watched Elizabeth walk to the baby carriage. The heat was getting to her. Perspiration dampened her flushed skin, made her blouse cling in all the right places, created havoc with her hair. The view from the back as she bent over the buggy made a man think. Slender, with long legs, she didn't know what a feast she was to the eyes. He ran a hand through his hair and shook his head. Maybe it was his self-imposed famine that was getting to him. Maybe malnourishment made a cactus look as desirable as a rose.

His gaze dropped again to her legs. He didn't know what she did for exercise, but she was in good shape. He figured squash or racquetball, one of those executive sports you could play in the city. Sports that were played more for business than pleasure. As far as he was concerned, that took all the fun out it. But then, he'd made his choices a long time ago. And they didn't include boardrooms, stock options, or thirty-story office buildings.

Elizabeth checked the baby. Mac had tucked her in the buggy and parked it in the deep shade of a maple tree just a few feet away from the table. Caroline's eyes were closed and she was sucking furiously on her thumb. No point in mentioning that to Mac. Again. She'd read all about thumb sucking and what it did to a child's teeth. When she'd mentioned it to him, he'd been totally unconcerned. Not to worry, he'd said. Several of his sister's kids had been thumb suckers and there'd been no problems. She'd cited authorities on the subject and he'd simply laughed and asked what she'd do to stop it—short of removing the thumb. It seemed to her just another example of how her book learning on the care of babies bore little, if any, resemblance to the real thing.

She rocked the carriage gently. She didn't want to leave Caroline. She wanted to be with her. She wanted to take her home. But Mac was back—and back to stay. Naturally, she'd be leaving. But surely Mac would understand that she'd taken two weeks off work just to be with her niece and would agree to give her at least that amount of time with her niece. Turning away from the baby, she returned to the table and sat across from Mac.

"Is she asleep?"

Nodding, she pulled off her glasses and rubbed the bridge of her nose. A dull throbbing had begun at her temples. What she feared, of course, was his reaction to her request. He'd certainly object. He had before. She lifted her glasses and sucked in a breath of the steamy air. Somehow, she'd find a way to convince him.

Mac watched her thick, spiky lashes sweep her cheeks as she closed her eyes, then opened them, and looked directly into his. The voltage in that brilliant blue sent a charge right through him. He shifted uncomfortably in his seat and prayed she'd stick those specs of hers back on, pronto.

Fortunately she did. And she slicked back her hair, straightened her collar, squared her shoulders, and cleared her throat. He knew it was reckoning time.

"Mac."

"Hmm?"

She cleared her throat again.

"Mac?"

"Yep?" He was patience itself.

"Mac, I've been thinking. I realize you're home now. I mean, I know the fishing trip is called off. And of course, you'll be home."

She was floundering. Badly.

She wanted to take Caroline home with her. She didn't know how to ask him.

He knew she wanted time with Caroline. He wasn't sure he should ask her to stay.

"Of course."

"And, of course, I'll be leaving."

"Of course."

He wasn't going to make this easy. He'd fished a baseball cap out of his back pocket and stuck it on his head. It sat low on his forehead, shading—and hiding—his eyes. She gritted her teeth. Why couldn't he say something polite like, "I know you were enjoying being with Caroline. Wouldn't you like to take her home for a few days?"

The sun was beating down on her back. Sweat was pooling and running down her neck. She was feeling a little hurt, or a little mad, or a little hot. Or all of the above.

Maybe she needed to wait until they were back at the house.

Maybe she needed to collect her thoughts.

When she suggested they leave, he didn't offer a single objection.

Maybe she was a great big chicken, she thought as they walked homeward. She'd never been afraid to speak her mind, never hesitated to go after what she wanted. And yet her eyes slanted toward Mac pushing the baby carriage, whistling softly under his breath. She found herself nearly tongue-tied around this man.

Not wanting to disturb the baby sleeping blissfully in her buggy, they decided to stay out on the front porch. Mac fixed iced tea and she sat on the porch swing while he slouched in a lawn chair with frayed webbing and a rusty frame. She couldn't help thinking what she'd do if this porch was hers. A fresh coat of paint, wicker furniture, potted plants, a rocking horse for Caroline. She could just picture it. Of course, it wasn't her porch. Or her house. And Caroline wasn't old enough to sit astride anything. And Mac could certainly live any way he liked.

She swirled the tea around in the glass, took a swallow, and tried to figure out a proper timetable. It was obvious she couldn't take Caroline home with her today. She had none of the things in her home that her niece would need. But she did know of a furniture company that specialized in baby things that could deliver most of it in a hurry. With a little planning and a shopping trip, she could be ready for Caroline in two to three days. She'd eliminate the need to convince Mac by presenting him with a fait accompli.

"I'll be leaving this afternoon, Mac."

Her voice broke the summer quiet like the sudden blast of an alarm. Mac flinched. Okay, she was leaving.

No reason for her not to, other than Cappy.

No reason he shouldn't want her to, other than Cappy.

He snuck a look at her from under the bill of his cap. Not a hair out place, blouse buttoned to her chin, all prim and proper. She'd be a really fun housemate, he thought sarcastically. He stifled the groan that rose in his throat. Okay, he could tell her she could stay. Sure, and he could check in with a shrink too. It was crazy, plumb crazy. He tipped back his cap, unhooked his leg from the arm of the chair, and sighed. He was actually going to do it.

"You don't have to leave, Elizabeth."

"I don't?"

"Nope."

"I don't think staying in a motel is a good solution, Mac. I can't possibly take care of Caroline there." It was an enormous effort to smile, but she did. She was not, she vowed, going to let Mac snatch the upper hand again.

"I wasn't talking about a motel."

"You weren't?"

"No." Boy, he really did need his head examined! They could barely communicate. "I meant you could stay on here, Elizabeth."

"Here?" Her smile failed her—and the all-too-familiar feeling of confusion crept into her brain like a mist.

"Yes."

"Are you going somewhere?"

"I hadn't planned on it."

"Then why would I stay at your house?"

It was a good question. Why indeed?

The baby started to make little snuffling noises, and Elizabeth hurried to the buggy. Caroline stopped crying and her tiny, rosebud mouth wavered into a smile.

"You'd stay because you want to be with Cappy."

Elizabeth didn't know whether it was the smile or the fat tear that hovered at the tip of her niece's nose that did it. She sucked in a breath, turned her head, and looked over her shoulder at Mac. "Well, I suppose I could stay." She wiped the tear away with the tip of her finger. "But just for a night or two."

She did know, though, that her decision had nothing to do with Mac. Absolutely nothing. That went without saying.

And, she reassured herself, she could just as easily call the furniture company from here. And do at least some of the shopping. In the meantime, she'd still be with Caroline. That was all she really wanted.

Chapter Five

Mac peeked into the kitchen, grimaced, then fled to the relative safety of the front porch with Cappy bouncing on his hip. He should have known. Elizabeth couldn't cook to save her life.

"It's not going to be a gourmet meal, I'll tell you that," Mac whispered to the baby. There were too many things boiling and burning in there. He had smelled the problem before he even went to the kitchen.

"And you should see that aunt of yours. She isn't looking real happy." As a matter of fact, she was looking pretty frazzled. The baby burped, none too softly, and he grabbed the cloth diaper he'd thrown over his shoulder and caught the dribble before it hit her chin. Jostling her around right after she ate was asking for it. He sat down gingerly and nestled her in his arms.

''What we've got here, Cap, is a lady without a domestic bone in her body.'' Colleen came padding up the steps and flopped down near his feet. He guessed Elizabeth had banished her from the kitchen. Considering what was going on in there, he didn't blame her. He wouldn't want any witnesses, either. ''And I think old Coll is going to make out tonight. There's sure to be lots of leftovers.''

The baby yawned and closed her eyes. Why not? Her tummy was full and it was her bedtime.

But whether Cappy knew it or not, Mac knew for sure that the lady was trying too hard, way too hard. He stared vacantly out at the quiet street. What he couldn't figure out was why. All he knew was that something wasn't playing quite right. Successful career woman wants to have custody of niece because she thinks the kid needs a female role model? No. It didn't play right at all. His gut told him that. But to find out what was really motivating her was going to be as tough as digging a hole in the tundra along about the middle of January. And maybe he wouldn't want to know. He exhaled heavily. Nah, no point kidding himself. He *did* want to know. Because she was still getting to him. Like an itch that wouldn't go away until it was scratched, he had to find out just what made Elizabeth tick.

He hauled himself out of the chair and carried his niece to her crib. Smells of disaster were still coming from the kitchen as he walked down the hall. He tucked the baby under the quilt and went to lower the shade. He had seen a bit of a thaw in Elizabeth, though. With Cappy. And when swinging, for a minute or two. But with him there hadn't been the first signs of defrosting. Grinning, he pulled the shade down. There was more than one way to skin a cat—or melt ice. He heard Elizabeth calling to him and the grin became a chuckle. It was a little unfair, this plan of his. But then, she was one tough lady.

Mac doused the rice on his plate with more soy sauce. It clung to his fork like glue as he lifted it to his mouth. It was just a tad more palatable than the chicken that tasted as dry and tough as old leather. But not much. Truth was, the whole darn meal was sitting in the pit of his stomach like a lead ball and his attempts to finish it were taking on heroic dimensions.

But there was nothing heroic about watching Elizabeth. The normally supercool, self-possessed lady sitting across the table from him wasn't looking any too poised now. Her blouse was stained from her efforts in the kitchen, her hair had pulled loose from its band

and curled wildly around her face, and her eyes were way too sparkly and bright. She'd taken three bites of her meal, murmured something about not being hungry, and had gulped down two glasses of water.

Across the table, Elizabeth cleared her throat. ''I think one of us needs to check on the baby.''

Mac shook his head. Hadn't he heard this before? Like all day long. He'd tried to tell her that Cappy had a set of lungs on her that would bring help from up to two blocks away.

She'd countered by reeling off a list of possible horrors she'd read about in one of those books she'd brought with her. He was beginning to think it was a darn good thing he'd come home when he did. She'd have been a basket case in under a week.

''We just checked on her fifteen minutes ago, Elizabeth. She's fine. I promise you.''

He was absolutely right, of course. What she'd really had in mind was some diversion, something to take her mind—and his—off the meal she'd prepared. It was too late to wish she'd agreed with Mac when he'd suggested ordering in Chinese food. They were both stuck with the dinner she'd prepared. And it was terrible. Horrible. And Mac was trying his best to eat what she couldn't. He was that polite. That much of a gentleman. Her eyes misted. The exhaustion of taking care of the baby must really be getting to her, she thought.

Mac laid his fork across his plate and tipped back in his chair. Elizabeth's chin rested in her hand and her eyes were wide over the rim of her glasses. He hoped it wasn't his imagination that had him convinced she was looking at him just a little differently: a little sweeter, softer. Now was the time. Before she'd take off to check on Caroline or before he changed his mind. Pushing back his chair, he stood. "Why don't we go out and sit on the porch?"

"What a good idea, Mac." She was mildly shocked at the words that came out of her mouth. Then not shocked at all. She smiled at Mac, at dear, sweet Mac. There simply wasn't a single thing pretentious about him—nothing phony or slick, she told herself, watching him walk toward her. He was, quite simply, rock-solid real. The wonder of it, she thought bemusedly as she rose from her chair, was that she hadn't realized it sooner. And sitting on the porch sounded lovely. And so she told him.

"Right." He couldn't help grinning. It was her sheer exhaustion talking, he knew it. He tucked her arm in his and led her out to the porch. But it was a nice change. A very nice change.

When he'd settled her on the swing, he sat down beside her instead of taking a seat in the lawn chair. It wasn't premeditated. He swore it wasn't. And he didn't actually put his arm around her. It was resting on the back of the swing. And in a minute or two he'd go back in the house for coffee.

The night was still warm and the stars were thick and Mac was a comforting presence by her side. More than comforting. Elizabeth's thoughts were a little muddled but she felt an absolute need to give him more of an explanation for that perfectly awful dinner. She wanted him to understand why it had been so awful. For reasons that weren't entirely clear to her, that had become very important. "Mac, I really do want to apologize for the . . . dinner. I should have told you I can't cook. As a matter of fact, I've *never* cooked."

"Never?" His brows rose in disbelief and he laughed. "Are you telling me you eat out all the time?"

She nodded. "Mostly. Or carryout, of course."

Incredulous, he continued, "Come on now, Elizabeth, didn't your mother teach you to cook?" He was almost sure she'd inched slightly closer and he let his arm shift so that his hand rested lightly on her shoulder.

"My mother?" There was an edge to her voice, a subtle change in the tone. "No. She didn't teach me."

Something wasn't right. She'd stiffened up. Her words were clipped and she followed them up with a short, low laugh. And in that laugh he'd heard pain, a pain he wanted to understand, a pain he suddenly wanted to erase.

His hand closed around her arm and he pulled her closer to his side. And met with no resistance. In the pale light of the moon her hair had lost the fire the sunlight gave it. But her skin was the color of pearls and her scent was heady in a way that made him grin. He'd never thought the smells of burnt food and perfume could make his heart leap. But it did. Until he felt the tremor run through her as their bodies touched, her shoulder against his arm, their knees touching. An actual tremor, as if she were afraid. As if closeness was an enemy.

He had a gut feeling her mother was the key that would unlock the enigma that was Elizabeth. He was sure of it. Although he knew he had no right to ask about the lady, he would— but gently, and fully prepared to back off if she wanted him to.

''So you and your mother ate out all the time too?'' He meant it as a joke, said it in jest, hoping she'd open up a bit.

''Childhood was a long time ago, Mac.'' She hesitated. Why say more? She'd never said more. Mac said nothing, but his presence, his easy silence, spoke volumes. She watched the fireflies, twinkling like stars fallen low, and heard the chirrup of a tree frog. All the while, Mac gently rocked them. ''I spent most of it in boarding schools.'' Her voice was nearly a whisper. ''My mother didn't cook.'' Her mouth curved in a half smile. ''That poor woman has had nearly as many cooks as husbands.''

''Husbands, plural?'' The words slipped out inadvertently. It was none of his business. He pulled her closer and she didn't resist.

''Oh my, yes. At last count, it was seven. At least I think so. She may very well have found another one by now.'' She hesitated.

Mac waited.

''Unfortunately, my mother collects husbands the way some people collect antique cars . . . or . . . or thimbles.'' She knew she was talking too much, confiding things she'd never confided to anyone. It had to be the fatigue that had loosened her tongue. Maybe. She was tucked in so close to Mac, she could feel his pulse, strong and steady, like the man himself.

Ah, there it was, Mac thought. The sadness he felt was an ache in his gut. The mother. And what of the little girl? She couldn't have felt wanted, loved. ''I'm sorry, Elizabeth,'' he said, because it was all he could say.

''Please don't misunderstand, Mac.'' She pulled out of the comforting circle of his arm. ''It was a blessing in disguise, really. It taught me to be independent, self-reliant. It made me see, early on, how important an education was, a career was. It saved me—'' She stopped abruptly. She'd almost said it had saved her from becoming like her mother, idly spinning out her years, looking only for the flattery of men, useless and used.

He was beginning to understand. More than understand. And he'd have to be careful about what he said and how he said it. She was much too proud and still too private to want sympathy or discussion. He moved his hand to the back of her neck and his fingers brushed gently across the small hollow at the base of her head. "What I think, Elizabeth, is that Cappy is lucky to have you for an aunt."

Of all the things he could have said, or was afraid he might say, that simple sentence took her breath away. Her eyes welled up with tears and her throat constricted. She turned her head away from him. "Thank you," she murmured.

"I said it because I meant it." With his other hand he reached for her chin and turned her to face him. "I hope you believe that, Elizabeth."

She'd never felt so vulnerable, so open—or so scared. His hands were rough, warm, and oddly comforting. And then the comfort was gone as his fingers threaded caressingly through her hair. Though the air was summer-hot, she felt a different kind of heat, a slow burn that inched down her spine. Emotions, some raw and painful, some tender and touching, warred within her. The man at her side had done what no other man had done, What she'd allowed no other man to do—he'd gotten a glimpse of her soul. Every instinct she had cried out for her to bar the gate, to close him out.

But how did you lock someone out who had found the key? The answer was crystal clear. You changed the locks.

His finger traced the line of her jaw, her lips, and then ever so slowly, he lowered his head and brushed her mouth with his. It was only barely a kiss. In the washed-silver light of the moon, his eyes were smoke gray, his face shadowed. He smelled of summer and something earthy and basic and his touch was sensuous and sure. Tomorrow, she thought, surely tomorrow was soon enough to change the locks.

And then he kissed her. Lightly at first, his lips soothing, seeking. Yet she felt the restraint, the control, as he waited for her response. He would go no further without her permission. She raised her arms and circled his neck and returned his kiss. For just this moment, this single moment, in the velvet and enveloping dark of a hot summer night, she would hold nothing back from this kiss.

He could hold her in his arms like this forever. But not now. Not tonight. Not on the heels of her confidences, not when he had the emotional advantage. He'd feel like a heel. Gently he pulled away and sighed deeply. His eyes met hers, and he pulled her closer again.

Elizabeth snuggled against him, with trust, with such wonder. Wonder at herself, for these new feelings. Wonder at this man who held her in the protective wrap of his arms. His heart thumped beneath her hand, his chin rested on the top of her head, his body heat enveloped her like a heady perfume. She'd never known such peace or felt such completeness.

The porch swing squeaked, insects thrummed and rasped, and the dog, stretched out on the mat by the door, yawned twice and rolled over. The sounds grew fainter, her eyes closed, and she fell asleep in his arms.

Once again, Mac stood at his bedside, staring down at a sleeping Elizabeth. He'd gently led her off the porch and inside the house insisting that she use his room again. He could always sleep on the couch. And now he marveled at the change in her. The polar cap was melting, the coldness gone. At least for tonight. Of course, she'd apologized profusely for falling asleep on the porch. When he'd told her it hadn't bothered him a bit, he knew she didn't hear him. Elizabeth didn't know how to give herself a break.

She sighed deeply in her sleep now and rolled onto her back. Mac bent closer, drawn as helplessly to her as a moth was to a flame. His lips brushed her forehead, his hand touched her hair. Enough, he told himself. Carefully, he pulled the sheet around her shoulders and started to tiptoe out, about to close the door behind him.

But just as he'd started to leave the room, she'd raised her head and said very softly, ''Thanks for everything, Mac.''

His voice had choked as he'd said good night.

Lying on the couch with his feet dangling over the end, he yawned and closed his eyes. He needed sleep and it wasn't going to come easily. He couldn't get his mind off the lady down the hall.

Some pieces of the puzzle had fallen into place. Given Elizabeth's childhood, he understood why she'd wanted custody of Cappy. Her motives weren't great for either Elizabeth or her niece, but he had a feeling he didn't need to point that out to her. He figured she'd come to that realization herself. And once she did, she'd then be free to love her niece for herself.

He clasped his hands behind his head and sighed deeply, the stream of air whistling softly through his lips. Elizabeth. He grinned. First impressions sure could be deceiving. He'd thought her the coldest woman he'd ever met, a real ice princess. He knew now that it was nothing but a facade, a facade of frost to hide behind, to keep others at a chilly distance. But . . . an analysis of Elizabeth didn't quite answer the question of why he lay there sleepless. His mouth parted in a smile of self-derision. *Come on, McAllister. You aren't her kind of man at all. And, in spite of your new-found understanding of her, she's not your kind of woman.*

He scrunched up the pillow behind his head. It was kind of like baseball. They were in different leagues entirely. But like a pickup game in a vacant lot, he could enjoy the few innings they'd have together.

Chapter Six

Elizabeth stepped out of the shower, somewhat revived. She'd awakened at seven in the morning, fully clothed and full of guilt. She knew why, knew herself well enough to know it was time to make a decision. Or more correctly, discard an old one. She towel dried quickly and pulled on a pair of shorts and a crisply ironed blouse. Her mouth quirked up. Ridiculous, inappropriate, these clothes of hers. She ran a brush through her hair and tied it loosely back. One hug, one burp, and the blouse would be a mess. A sharp stab of longing, of yearning, struck like a body blow. She wrapped her arms around her waist and waited for the pain to ease. It was time. Time to go back where she came from. Time to return home and leave these two people alone. Her heart was beating much too fast and the palms of her hands were damp as she entered the kitchen.

The room smelled of warm milk and coffee. Mac had a towel hanging apronlike from his waist and a piece of toast in his hand. The baby was blowing bubbles, her eyes nearly crossed in concentration. A wide, bright band of sunlight laid itself across the room like a cloth on a table.

Both of them smiled at her. Killer smiles. Kind smiles. They pierced her heart like knives. She smiled back—too bright, too cheery, so false. And went straight to the coffeepot.

Mac munched his toast thoughtfully. He'd cued in to that smile and knew there was something afoot. He checked his watch. He didn't want to think what it might be. And right now he couldn't. He was running late. "Elizabeth, I forgot to to tell you last night that Cappy has a checkup this morning. Do you want to come with us?"

"Oh, thank you, Mac, but I have some things I need to get done." A reprieve! A little time to work out the telling, the farewell. She kept her back to him, fussing unnecessarily with a spoon and cream.

"Okay. It'll be a couple of hours though. Dr. Marian is the only pediatrician in town and she has to triple book just to see everyone.'' He tossed the towel on the back of a chair. Elizabeth was stirring the heck out of the coffee. And not looking at him. *Who're you kidding, Mac?* He knew darn well what she was up to. And it felt like he'd just taken a punch in the gut—a punch he should've seen coming. His jaw tightened and he reached down and picked up his niece. He'd have to deal with it later. ''I think short stuff wants to say good-bye.''

Mac held out Caroline and Elizabeth took her in her arms and held her close. She smelled of powder and pablum. Her red ringlets were pulled into a topknot and held in place by a tiny pink bow. Dimpled fingers clutched at her blouse. She brushed a kiss on the baby's forehead and another on the tip of her nose. And as Elizabeth handed her back to Mac, Caroline gurgled, burbled, and spoke. ''Ma-ma,'' she said. There was no mistaking it and the word pierced like a cupid's arrow, straight to her heart. Her hand went to her chest, her eyes to Mac. He was busy untying the bib from the baby's neck. It seemed he hadn't heard, though the word was clear as a bell to her own ears.

''We'll be back as soon as we can. I've left the bread out and there's eggs in the fridge.''

''Thanks.'' She blinked away the sudden tears in her eyes and followed them to the front door.

Mac propped the screen open with his foot and turned back toward Elizabeth. Her skin had a morning glow to it, her hair was a halo of gold-red around her face, and she smelled better than a bunch of freshly picked flowers. He knew all too well what she was up to—and he knew he couldn't do a thing about it. His thumb slid under her chin and tilted it up. ''Don't you go anywhere, okay?'' His lips brushed her mouth and then he was gone. Out the door, down the steps, afraid to look back.

Elizabeth grasped the door frame, weak-kneed, light-headed, numb. It wasn't just the kiss, but what he said. He knew she was leaving. How he knew, she couldn't say. She banged the door shut. That man could read her as no one else ever had. As if— She chuckled out loud in the empty house. As if he had second sight.

Hands on her hips, she surveyed the room. Well, there was one surprise she had in mind Mac wouldn't know, couldn't guess. She marched to the kitchen and started hauling out cleaning supplies. She pulled the vacuum into the living room and plugged it in. She'd promised herself she'd do a little tidying up before she left—and she was going to leave, first thing tomorrow.

As for her niece—she pushed the button on the vacuum and it roared to life. *Just clean,*

Elizabeth, she told herself, *and don't think about Caroline for a while.* She shoved the couch away from the wall. And Mac? The couch rammed into the end table and the lamp teetered, nearly falling to the floor before she grabbed it. The seesawing lamp that she rescued mirrored the state of her emotions. Sinking to her knees, she buried her face in her hands. At this moment, she wished she'd never laid eyes on either one of them. It was too painful—the knowing, the loving, the leaving. She'd fallen in love with her niece. Tears trickled between her fingers, hot and salty. And she was falling in love with Mac.

Somehow she heard the phone over the noise of the vacuum. She swiped, hastily, at the tears on her face and grabbed the receiver on the sixth ring.

"Elizabeth. Hi. It's Kate."

"Hello, Kate." She hoped there was no telltale sign of tears in her voice.

"Oh, I am so glad I reached you! I ran over to Dr. Marian's this morning to pick up Ted's allergy medicine and Mac and the baby were there and Mac told me you were thinking of leaving tomorrow and I'm so hoping you won't."

She knew it. Mac had guessed right. But she wasn't thinking about leaving. She *was* leaving—bright and early in the morning. Without Caroline. Without sending for Caroline. The lump was back in her throat and she swallowed hard before answering. ''Well, I really do need to get back. Besides, now that Mac is home, there's no reason for me to stay.''

''Oh, but there *is* a reason for you to stay, Elizabeth. We're going to have a picnic tomorrow and we'd love for you to come. I know it's last-minute. I just never seem to be able to plan these things in advance. I hope you don't mind?''

There was a reason to stay. Elizabeth's heart upped its tempo and her grip tightened on the phone. *All right,* she acknowledged silently, *it's an excuse parading as a reason. But it'll do.* Her lips parted and she smiled. *It'll do just fine.*

''Heavens no, Kate. I don't mind. And I'd love to come. It's so nice of you to include me. I'll postpone leaving for one more day. Just tell me what I can bring.''

''Oh, goodness.'' Kate laughed. ''We're doing chicken and corn on the cob. Just anything or nothing. It's you we want.''

After thanking Kate, Elizabeth hung up the phone slowly. She knew that every word Kate said was heartfelt and genuine. It was she who felt like a fraud. What she needed, really needed, was to get back to reality. Her reality. The reality that reminded her of who she was and where she belonged. No dreams, no wishful thinking. And love had everything to do with it. To love enough to let go, to let live. She picked up the vacuum handle, flipped the switch, and attacked the living room rug. But surely one more day wouldn't matter, couldn't hurt. And she'd bring fresh fruit. That she could handle.

Two hours later, she'd finished everything but the kitchen floor. Mac had completed most of the unpacking before she'd arrived and with the bookcases filled, pictures hung, and the rooms cleaned, it was becoming a home. She wandered into the den and stood before a wall covered with framed pictures of young boys in yellow-and-black football gear and young girls in blue-and-white softball uniforms. Their faces were lit with proud, broad smiles, though none was prouder or broader than the smile of their coach, standing at their side.

She touched a frame with the tip of her finger. It was an affirmation, an acknowledgement that she'd made the right decision. She left the room quickly, her eyes stinging, her throat tight.

Filling a bucket with sudsy water, she dipped in the mop and began to scrub the kitchen floor. If there was one thing she'd learned as a child, it was how to clean. Home between school terms and camps, she'd been left with the maids, who'd discovered a more than willing worker. She wondered if any of them had guessed it was companionship she'd wanted. Someone to spend time with her. It helped, later, to understand her mother's endless searching—ever lonely, ever frightened of being alone.

She settled herself down on the back porch stairs, waiting for the floor to dry. Caroline would never know that kind of aching, hollow loneliness, thank goodness. The dog nudged her hand, begging for attention. *Nor will you,* she thought, as she wrapped her arm around Colleen's neck. The sun was hot and high, the cicadas were revving up, and a butterfly toe-danced near her feet. And finally, in the humid-heavy heat of Mac's weedy backyard, she allowed herself to think of last night.

It was a night of vulnerability, of risk. A night that, in recalling, both stung and soothed. She raised her knees to her chin and wrapped her arms around her legs. Eyes closed against the white glare of sun, she felt again the caress of Mac's mouth, of his hands, and of his voice, velvet soft in the cloaking darkness. He'd given her more than time—he'd given of himself. And she had taken, yet, in a small way, like a beginning swimmer learning to trust the water, she'd given too. But that wouldn't be enough for Mac—or for Caroline. They deserved more. They'd need a strong swimmer, for the waters they swam in were deeper than hers, slower-moving, broad and wide. She was out of her depth and she knew it. But she could thank them for allowing her to wade in, waist-high, heart-high, and revel in the cool currents and rippling eddies. The dog bumped her leg and she opened her eyes.

Colleen stood, ears pricked, tail raised, staring fixedly ahead. The squirrel was up the tree and chittering angrily from a high branch before the dog was halfway across the yard. Chuckling, Elizabeth rose and stretched. The dog hadn't stood a chance.

It occurred to her as she swung open the screen door that she hadn't called the office all week, hadn't even thought of the office. It didn't seem possible, for it was her life, her lifeblood. The wash of uneasiness she felt disturbed her. A feeling, faceless and still, lay just below the surface and she couldn't name it— or didn't want to.

She grasped the handle of the baby buggy parked on the porch, rocking it gently, and let her mind spool back in time. The picture that formed was of Mac hefting a squealing Caroline from the buggy, lifting her high above his head. Her hands tightened on the handle and she shook her head, bemused and amused at herself. She understood one thing very well. With those two, she hadn't stood a chance.

*   *   *

Mac swung open the front door and stepped in quietly. Cappy was asleep, her head heavy on his shoulder. The house was cool and dark, the blinds closed against the hot afternoon sun. He smelled lemon oil and soap as he headed for the baby's room. Tucking the sleeping baby into her crib, he walked slowly through the house.

He was astounded. Amazed. Puzzled.

Elizabeth couldn't cook, had never cared for a child, but she could clean? He honestly couldn't picture it. But she'd done a great job. The place shone, sparkled, glowed. A clean tablecloth was laid on the kitchen table, fresh towels in the bathroom. There wasn't a thing out of place. And there wasn't a sign of Elizabeth. But he knew she was here, for her car was out front and her suitcases were stacked neatly in his bedroom.

He'd called her from Kate's to say he'd be later than expected because when he'd stopped by his sister's he'd found her ankle-deep in water and thoroughly exasperated. The washing machine had overflowed and she couldn't get a repairman. Elizabeth had breezily said she understood, was busy herself. He'd pictured her at the table, briefcase open, papers stacked high. Not with a mop and a dust rag.

Three hours later, he'd left to come home.

There was only one place left to look. He opened the door to the back porch and stepped out. Elizabeth raised her head and stood as he came down the steps. Her face and knees were streaked with dirt, she was as sweaty as one of his players, and she looked as pleased as punch. The bushes were trimmed, the patio swept, and a dozen newly planted flowers added cheery color to the once bare earth. All he could do was stare.

Elizabeth cocked her head and grinned. If there was one word to describe the look on Mac's face, dumbfounded would be it. The dog moved to her side, nosing her hand, wanting to share in the glory. And it was a glorious moment.

"I may not be able to cook, but I'm a darn good gardener."

"Yeah." He was still staring, open-mouthed and nearly speechless. "And the house, too. It's . . . it's—" He was at a loss for words.

"Sparkling? Picture perfect?" A bubble of laughter escaped her lips.

"All of the above." His grin matched hers and he took a step closer. She took a step back.

"Why, thank you." She dipped her head in a patently false show of modesty.

"No. It's I who needs to thank you." This time he took three steps, three long steps closer.

She stayed put.

"I wonder how I can."

"You already have."

He moved closer still until he was a mere foot away—just twelve inches, if that. His body blocked the sun, shading her like a sturdy tree. She couldn't have moved if she'd wanted to—and she didn't want to. His voice was husky and heavy. His eyes fastened on hers. "Not the way I want to."

"Well . . ." She couldn't meet his eyes, couldn't meet the truth she saw, the truth he was willing to let her see. A bead of perspiration trickled down her neck. A blade of grass tickled her ankle. A tremor of emotion ran the length of her spine. Her brain was whirling, her heart pumping.

She wanted to reach out to him.

She wanted to touch him.

She wanted to want, and not be afraid to let him know.

Instinct made her reach for her glasses. She settled them on her nose. *Keep it light. Keep it safe,* she told herself. She raised her eyes to his and smiled. "Do you know what I want?"

"Nope."

She kept smiling for all she was worth. "A garden hose."

"Ah." His lips quirked up and he watched her fool with those specs of hers and thought,

Elizabeth, Elizabeth. You're a terrible liar. Did you forget body language? Did you forget I got a glimpse of those blue eyes of yours without the glasses? But he understood and was even a little grateful. "Then you shall have a hose. Wait right here."

She watched him sprint across the yard and out the gate to the front of the house as her heartbeat thundered in her ears. Did he know how close she came to revealing her true feelings? Did he guess what was happening to her?

He returned with the hose coiled and looped over his broad shoulder. And when he fastened the hose to the spigot and turned it on, he grinned—like Peck's bad boy, like a kid up to no good.

There was no place to run, no place to hide, no way to outwit him. Elizabeth started to laugh. She shook her head and raised her hands in mock horror. "Don't," she protested feebly, not meaning it.

The water hit her knees first and the dirt ran down her legs in muddy rivulets, puddling beneath her feet. Mac kept it up, playing the hose like a conductor with a baton, waving it high, then low, then in looping, lazy circles, drenching her shoulder, her elbow, her hip. She backed away, sidled sideways, crablike, and turned her back to him.

Her laughter nearly doubled her over.

His laughter shook his whole frame.

Finally she had enough. She needed to change her tactics. A spray of water caught her in the chest as she whipped around to face him. Her eyes narrowed and sparked with pure, unadultered revenge.

With a shout she'd never thought she could make, she charged toward Mac, straight across the wet, slippery grass. He gave a whoop of surprise and defensively raised his arm, holding the hose high above his head, creating for the two of them their own summer shower.

Up on tiptoe, arms flailing like windmills as she tried to grab the hose, Elizabeth lost her balance. She jerked one arm down and thrust it toward Mac to stop herself from falling. She needn't have bothered, for Mac was lightning fast and before her hand reached him, he'd scooped her to his side, his arm circled around her, his hand splayed just below her rib cage. For a fraction of a second, she stiffened up, about to pull away, but she was out of breath, soaking wet, and ready to give up.

The water arced high above their heads and the sun made a mosaic of rainbows in the dancing, falling drops. Without allowing herself to think, she let her head rest in the crook of his shoulder. Her arm was wedged between them and she wriggled it free and inched it slowly around his waist and rested her hand gingerly on his hipbone.

Time played out in milliseconds. She heard the hiss of the water from the hose, the thud of her heartbeat, the fainter thump of Mac's, and the cicadas' ceaseless serenade.

Slowly, Mac let the hose drop from his hand. It hit the ground and slithered, snake-like, for a few seconds, the water tonguing its way across the grass. He shifted his weight to his other foot and turned, wrapping both his arms around the slender waist of Elizabeth Kincaid.

Her glasses were gone, bounced off in a moment neither one remembered. Her eyes were wide, the blue now darkened. Tiny beads of moisture trembled on her thick lashes. Her pulse throbbed in her throat. A tiny drop of water rolled to the tip of her nose, hovering, waiting for him to nudge it free. She raised her chin and her lips parted in a smile that gave him the courage—or the foolhardiness—to dislodge the droplet then move his mouth to hers.

Their skin was slick, their clothes sodden, their hair dripping. He kissed her on her nose, her mouth, and her temple.

Her skin was warm. Her nose was pink from sunburn, and her lips were soft.

He sighed deeply and pulled her closer. How it happened, he didn't know. Why it happened, he'd never know. But it had happened. He'd fallen in love with Elizabeth Kincaid. And she was leaving.

Chapter Seven

Elizabeth folded her nightgown and laid it in the suitcase. There was nothing left to pack. No further reason to delay. She closed the top, zipped it shut, and walked to the window. A summer storm had moved in during the night. The black-gray clouds made morning seem like dusk. The wind blew the rain in silver sheets across the yard, smacked it against the windowpane, pooled it on the street. Yesterday had been perfect. The picnic was a success, and Mac's family had been so friendly and welcoming.

She rested her head against the pane of glass. The sweet smell of baby powder clung to her like perfume. She felt as if she could still hear Caroline's crows of delight yesterday as one cousin after another begged to hold her. And she could still recall how the baby had raised her arms high, reaching out for Mac. Her niece had so many to love her.

A bolt of lightning scissored the sky, followed by a clap of thunder that shook the house. She pulled away from the window, shivering slightly, and reached for her raincoat. It seemed so strange, now, that she'd actually thought Caroline should be with her. Surrounded by family, yet with a home of her own, Caroline was just fine exactly where she was. She would want for nothing that was important. Elizabeth lifted the suitcase off the bed and left the room.

After leaving her luggage by the front door, she went to the kitchen. Mac was at the table, hidden behind the morning newspaper. Caroline was in her swing, dozing. A bluegrass band on the radio played softly in the background.

Mac heard her come into the kitchen and sucked in a ragged breath. It was time.

''Mac?''

Her voice was a whisper. It could have been a bellow the way it shook him to the core. He lowered the paper slowly. ''Yes?''

''I'm leaving now.'' She smiled brightly and consulted her watch. As if she had a timetable of some sort. As if she was pressed for time.

It was a charade that would fool no one, least of all her, but it would keep her moving.

Mac folded the paper with meticulous care and laid it on the table. "You don't have to leave, you know." He'd say it again as he had last night. They both knew what her answer would be.

"Oh, Mac. I do." She fumbled with the buttons of her coat. She couldn't look at him. She went to the swing and bent to the baby. "But I'll be back to visit." She kissed the baby's forehead and touched her cheek. Caroline slept on, blissfully unaware of her aunt's imminent departure. Tears blurred her vision as she whispered softly, "Good-bye, sweetheart."

Mac rose from the chair, curbing the impulse to reach for her. He'd spent most of the night lying awake wondering how he could let her go, knowing he couldn't keep her. "I'll take your bags to the car."

"Thank you." She followed him silently from the kitchen. She was doing the right thing . . . the right thing. Over and over, like a mantra, a prayer, she repeated those three simple words. She gathered up her purse, her umbrella, a carryall. Mac swung open the front door and stood aside for her.

Elizabeth stopped abruptly at the top of the porch stairs and laid a restraining hand on Mac's arm. "Wait a minute. Let me put up the umbrella or you'll get drenched."

"A little water won't hurt me." His face was a study in concern. "But you shouldn't be driving in this mess."

"I'll be fine. I'll take it slowly." Elizabeth opened her umbrella, holding it high, shielding the two of them from the downpour as their stilted, polite phrases gave them the protection they needed from themselves.

He lifted her bag higher on his shoulder. His smile was strained. "Okay, then. Let's go."

It took just a few moments to deposit the luggage in the trunk. Ducking back under her umbrella, Mac grasped her by the shoulder as she opened the car door. "Call me when you get home, okay? I want to know you made it safe and sound."

His hand was heavy on her shoulder, his brow ridged with concern. She couldn't trust herself to answer. Nodding, she slid into the car.

"We'll miss you, Elizabeth." There was a hollowness in his voice that matched the bleakness she felt. Unable to respond, she watched silently as he collapsed the umbrella, placed it on the seat behind her, and closed the door.

Her hand was shaking as she turned the key in the ignition. Pulling away from the curb, she raised her other hand in a brief farewell. Shifting into second gear, she sought him out in the rearview mirror. He was standing in the middle of the street, legs planted wide, soaking wet, watching her leave.

"Oh, Mac." Her voice choked on the words; tears spilled down her face. "I'll miss you and Caroline too."

Two weeks. She'd been back home for two weeks. Elizabeth peeled out of her suit jacket, kicked off her shoes, and padded across the Oriental carpet. Caroline smiled out at her from the silver frame sitting atop the piano. Her finger traced the frame, the line of the baby's face. There were other pictures, a stack of them, not inches away. Photos taken at the picnic. Snapshots of Caroline—and Mac. She hadn't touched them since she'd had them developed. And she didn't touch them now. She wouldn't. In truth, she couldn't. The longing she felt was as raw as an open wound—and one didn't rub salt in an open wound.

Abruptly she turned and went to the kitchen.

She put water on to boil then went for her mail. But she'd call them tonight, she decided as she flipped through the pile of magazines, bills, and flyers. Once a week was perfectly reasonable. She was Caroline's aunt. She was family. And Mac had agreed. She went through the mail one more time. Nothing from her mother. She tossed the pile on the desk and returned to the kitchen. Not that she expected anything. Not this soon. She took the whistling, steaming kettle from the burner and fixed a cup of tea.

It was only two weeks since she'd sent her mother a long letter and pictures of her grand-daughter. And overseas mail, unless sent by an express service, still took an inordinately long time. Sitting at the kitchen table, she propped her elbows on the smooth wood and cupped the mug of hot tea in her hands.

Her eyes strayed to the clock on the wall. Six o'clock. Mac would be feeding Caroline. The radio would be on. And coffee, a fresh pot. The dog would be nearby. She reached for the phone and punched in the numbers. Eight rings. Eight long rings and then the answering machine clicked on. She hung up quickly, before Mac's voice came on the line asking the caller to leave a message. It was an impulsive action that made her feel silly and immature. But she knew why. She didn't want to hear his voice.

She drummed her fingers on the table. To-night was an at-home night, a night to wash clothes, take a long bath, and give herself a manicure. Tomorrow evening she had a date with Brad. He had tickets for the symphony. He'd picked out a new restaurant for them to try. She'd had to make herself accept his in-vitation. She rose from the table and paced the room. No sense in staying home. She'd go to a movie, then stop for some Chinese food on the way home.

She moved swiftly, changing into slacks and a blouse, taking a sweater in case the air-conditioning was too cold. As she shut the front door, she remembered the lamb chop she'd moved from the freezer to the fridge this morning. She'd been doing a little cooking since she'd returned home, Simple things like chops, salads, and baked potatoes.

Her car purred to life and she pulled the seat belt across her chest. *Cooking? Whatever for, Elizabeth?* For a brief period of time she'd been transported into another world, a world where the mundane, the commonplace, seemed mysterious and magical. That interlude was over, behind her. Her life didn't include cooking, or a baby with a milk-smeared mouth and dimpled cheeks—or a man with a baseball cap pulled low over laughing, gray eyes.

Her chest felt tight, her throat dry and parched. Caroline and Mac were a pair, a duo, in a close and closed circle of family. For a short while she'd been drawn into their orbit. But it was their orbit, not hers. She needed to remember that.

Stopped at a red light, she realized she had no recollection of driving this far. The movie theater was now just half a block away. So much for reverie, she thought wryly and with a modicum of fear. And so much for self-pity.

She had a full and fulfilling life, enriched now by her niece. For that she should be more than grateful.

As she entered the theater, a man in a baseball cap crossed in front of her. It wasn't Mac. She knew it wasn't, yet she nearly called out his name. In the darkened theater, with the curtain slowly rising and the smell of popcorn buttery strong, she saw a scene as clearly as if it was the film itself—Mac, bare feet propped on a table, a baby dangling on his knee and a bowl of popcorn balanced on the other. Her eyelids prickled with unshed tears. *Stop this,* she pleaded silently with herself. Shoving her glasses up on her nose, she willed herself back to the present and focused on the screen.

''Are you going to take me with you when you move upstairs?'' Peggy tossed off the question with the all the assurance of one who knew she was needed and would never be left behind.

Elizabeth looked over the top of her glasses and smiled. ''*If* I move upstairs, you mean. And honestly, I don't know why you bother to ask. As if I could get along without you.''

''Well, you may have to fight over me. That new woman, Ellen Stanton, has been making overtures, you know.''

''This wouldn't be a clever ploy for a raise, would it?''

"Heaven forbid, I should be so crass." Peggy sniffed self-righteously. "Though I must say, you've been so absentminded lately, I was getting a little worried. Not, of course, about myself, but about you."

Elizabeth's eyes had strayed to a picture of Caroline she'd framed and brought to her office. At lunchtime today, she'd found a tiny pair of sandals she thought might fit her niece's chubby feet. Though, according to Mac, her niece was growing daily and— She started and looked up. Peggy was still talking to her! Guiltily, she focused on her secretary, hoping Peggy hadn't noticed her lack of attention.

"And I hardly think you can blame me!"

"Well, um, no. Of course not," Elizabeth murmured noncommitally. It didn't seem to be quite enough, for Peggy's mouth was still pursed in pique. "But thank you," she added quickly, then flipped closed the folder that lay on her desk and consulted her watch. "Let's call it a day, Peg, and go home."

"And that's another thing. I've never known you to get out of here before seven at the very earliest. But ever since you've come back from your vacation, or whatever those couple of days off were, you're gone no later than quarter of six. Not that I'm complaining, you understand. But. . . . " Peggy frowned. "Are you sure you're feeling all right?"

"I'm fine." She gathered up her purse and briefcase and smiled. "See you in the morning."

She heard Peggy mumble something about locking up her desk as she hurried out the door. She knew she was acting out of character and that her unusual behavior had her secretary concerned, yet she couldn't help it. She wasn't willing to tell Peggy she had to get home before Mac put Caroline to bed.

She punched the button for the elevator. *Ah, Elizabeth. That doesn't answer, at all, why you're leaving early the other four nights.* She fiddled with her glasses. She loved her job, her career. There was no question about it. But something had changed. Something inside her. For reasons she'd yet to understand fully, it was no longer all-consuming.

Once again the phone rang, eight long rings. This time she left a message. She pulled off her glasses and rubbed the bridge of her nose. A shudder of concern rippled through her. So they weren't home last evening or tonight. It didn't mean anything was wrong. Mac was probably coaching something and Caroline would be at Kate's, happy, healthy, and enjoying her cousins. She'd try again tomorrow.

She flipped on the radio and let the sound fill the room with the evening news. She couldn't have cared less. The only news she wanted was of Caroline. She walked toward the window, then stopped abruptly. Brad! He would be here in half an hour. She hurried toward her bedroom, unbuttoning her blouse and unhooking her skirt as she went.

Two minutes later, she arched back her neck and let the water from the shower pour over her. Eyes closed, she saw a garden and a hose held high and she and Mac, laughing, clinging to each other, wet to the bone. Her lips parted in a smile. Warmth. The warmth of his hand on hers, his mouth on her lips. And the indescribable, illogical, intoxicating warmth of Mac himself. Her sigh was long and despairing. She reached for the shampoo and bent her head.

Her dress was silk, her pearls flawless, her mood somber. She could not, would not compare the two men. It was blatantly unfair to Brad. She waited under the awning as he spoke with the valet and reminded herself again how much they had in common, how comfortable they were together, how this was the kind of man she enjoyed.

The maître d' led them to a table covered in heavy white linen, set with silver and crystal that glowed in the soft candlelight. The music and voices were subdued, the waiters deferential; the food would be perfect. There was nothing wrong with this. And yet there was everything wrong with this. She felt as cold as the bottle of champagne that rested in its bucket of ice.

"Welcome home, Elizabeth." Brad lifted his glass to her. "Where was it you went on vacation?"

"A small town a couple of hours from here. I doubt you'd know it. I was visiting my niece." She raised her glass and smiled at the man across from her. Home. He was right; she was home. Her vacation was over and what had happened had been like those shipboard romances she'd read of—never meant to last once ashore. But that only had to do with Mac, for her vacation had provided her with a treasure she'd never lose, would always have. A niece. A child she could love. Her hand covered the small beaded purse that lay on the table. Inside was her wallet with two photos of Caroline. "Would you like to see a picture of her?"

"Sure." Elizabeth detected the quick flicker of surprise in his eyes before he looked over her shoulder, signaling to the waiter.

Her hand withdrew from the purse and her mouth twisted slightly in a wry assessment of the situation. Hadn't she once been bored to the point of tears by parents keen on showing her stacks of pictures of their little darlings? She couldn't expect Brad to feel any differently. But now she, finally understood how those parents had felt. And she could always share all of her hopes and fears regarding her niece with Mac. She simply didn't need that from Brad.

She picked up the menu and scanned it quickly. "Actually, I don't think I brought any with me. Some other time, perhaps."

"Okay." The relief in his voice was unmistakable. Elizabeth felt herself relax. One more emotional hurdle, one more lesson to learn. And there wasn't a reason in the world not to enjoy herself. She was suddenly ravenous.

The red light on her answering machine was blinking when she got in. Perhaps it was her mother. She was notorious for calling late at night. Or was it Mac? Had he returned her call just minutes after she'd left? She kicked off her shoes and punched the answer button. It took a moment for the caller's name to register and when it did she stiffened, fear racing up her spine like a current of electricity.

"Elizabeth, it's Kate. I picked up Mac's messages for him and so I thought I'd better call you. Mac and Caroline are here with me. There was an accident. Now, everything will be all right, but Mac had the battery blow up in his face while working on that car of his. Some of the acid, thankfully just a little, got in his eyes. He'll be fine, but . . . but he's been temporarily blinded. The doctors assured us it'll clear up in no more than a couple of weeks, possibly sooner. We're so grateful it wasn't worse. But, please, don't worry. He's going to recover completely. Call anytime. Bye-bye.''

Elizabeth sank into the chair by her desk, stunned by the message she'd received. The machine beeped, warning her it was erasing the message. She started to reach for the phone, then stopped. She'd have to call information first because she didn't have Kate's number. And once she got it, then what? Offer her condolences? Send Mac a card? Flowers?

Her stomach roiled and she pressed her hands against her abdomen. Mac was hurt, blinded. Unable to see. Helpless and needing help. Tears glistened in her eyes. She wanted to offer to help, someway, somehow. But the question, of course, was—should she?

Chapter Eight

"You're not really going to leave?" Peggy gasped. Her eyebrows rose halfway up her forehead.

"I'm taking leave, some vacation time, Peg, not leaving. There is a difference, you know." Elizabeth stuffed a couple of file folders into her briefcase.

"Look, maybe it's none of my business, but Glynda said she heard you and Mr. Sanders really had a knock-down-and-drag-out. And what he said to her after you left would make your toes curl."

Elizabeth sighed. "He's being unreasonable, Peg. I haven't taken a day off in over three years and when I took some time off

125

recently, I was back sooner than I anticipated. I'm long overdue and he knows it.''

''Okay, okay. I understand all that. But wouldn't you agree your timing is lousy? You're up for a promotion, if you remember.''

''Peggy, let me make something clear. I'm not leaving for Club Med, or London, or to laze the days away in bed. There's been an emergency of sorts and I'm going to help out.'' She wasn't handling this well. She could tell that by the mutinous look on Peggy's face. Guilt niggled inside her. And how was Peg to understand, for Pete's sake? Sure, Peggy knew she had a niece, knew she'd gone to meet her, stay with her. But she'd given her secretary a heavily edited version of the events. And of Mac, Peg knew nothing at all.

She softened her voice. ''Philip may be upset, but he's aware of the nature of my leaving and I know that when he calms down, he won't give it another thought.''

''He won't give *you* another thought, is what you mean,'' Peggy muttered, just loudly enough for Elizabeth to hear.

She changed the subject, hoping to derail her secretary from the single track she seemed determined to stay on. She picked up a sheet of paper and held it out. ''I've made a list of a few things I need you to do while I'm away, Peg. As for my calendar, I've gone through it and contacted everyone personally, so you shouldn't have any problems with that. Oh, and I put a number where you can reach me, if you need to, on there also.''

Peggy snatched the paper from Elizabeth's hand and ran her eyes down the page.

''Any questions?''

''No. Thank you.'' Peggy spun around and marched out the door.

Ten minutes later, she opened the door and stuck her head in. ''Do you have a minute?''

Elizabeth smiled and nodded. ''I was just about to buzz for you.'' She waved her hand at the chair. ''Sit down, Peggy.''

''Oh, Elizabeth, I want to apologize for my outburst. I'm sorry. I know you've got some sort of family emergency and you should be there. I had no right . . . ''

''It's okay, Peggy. I need to apologize too for being so unfeeling. You were only thinking of my welfare and I want you to know how much I appreciate that.''

''Well, you deserve that promotion. More than anyone here.''

''Thanks for the vote of confidence.'' She leaned forward in her chair. ''I won't be gone longer than two weeks, Peg, and much as I hate to say it, no one is indispensable, including me. You'll all muddle through somehow, I'm sure.''

''Well . . . we'll try.'' Peggy stood and walked to the door. She didn't sound or look convinced, but she had the good sense to give up. "I'll be here if you need me."

Once Peggy was out the door, Elizabeth propped her chin in her hands and closed her eyes. Her head throbbed; her stomach felt queasy. There was yet another reason for both Peg's astonishment and Philip's anger. Besides her routine of working late, working weekends, and never taking vacations, she had a reputation for being less than understanding with staff who requested time off for what she refered to as "personal problems." She winced inwardly as she recalled her lectures about keeping one's private life out of the workplace.

Her phone beeped softly and as she reached to pick it up, she glanced at the picture of her mother sitting next to Caroline's on her desk. Chic straw hat, oversized sunglasses, and not a hint of a smile on her face. Behind her the ocean was a brilliant blue-green.

Elizabeth turned into the driveway of Kate's house and inched forward, stopping well before the litter of trikes, balls, a battered red wagon, and a lone in-line skate trailing a fluorescent orange lace. She reached for the door handle and hesitated. She knew her offer to come and help had been gratefully received by an overburdened but uncomplaining Kate. And though, at first, Mac had been resistant to the idea, he'd finally agreed. She had no doubt at all that he was very concerned about being a burden to his sister. She pushed up the handle, opened the car door, and hesitated. Her reluctance to get out of the car was born, she decided, out of her sense of inadequacy to the task at hand.

Slowly, she climbed out of the car and pushed the door shut, fear still nibbling at the edges of her consciousness. The neighborhood was unusually quiet, the sun wiltingly hot, the acrid smell of melting asphalt in the air. As her hand reached for the doorbell, she suddenly understood the source of her fear. It wasn't inadequacy that filled her with a dreading doubt, but intimacy.

His motives were rotten. Ulterior. Downright sneaky. Mac shifted on the couch and inhaled deeply. He could smell the faint medicinal odor of the bandages that covered his eyes, feel the weight of his grandfather's walking stick resting against his leg, and hear Elizabeth, back in the bedroom, crooning to their niece. He'd no right allowing her come. Sure, it was true that he felt keenly the extra work he and Cappy created for his sister. It was also true that he'd finally located a woman who'd agreed to live in and take care of the baby and himself until the bandages were removed.

He hunched forward on the couch. So why was it that when Elizabeth called and offered to come and help out he hadn't said one word to a living soul about the arrangements he'd made? Why was it he'd surreptitiously called the woman, when his sister was out of earshot, and told her she wouldn't be needed? Ah, the truth was— He grasped the arm of the couch as if the truth would send him flying. The honest, naked truth was he wanted to see Elizabeth again.

He chuckled softly. *Wrong choice of words, Mac,* he told himself. He could hear her, smell her, touch her, perhaps. He couldn't see her. Not for a while. His fingers rubbed against the fabric on the couch arm, exploring the weave, the ribbed nubbiness. But eventually he would see her. He was lucky. His blindness was temporary; the doctors had assured him of that. In the meantime, he hoped. What *did* he hope? He raised his head sharply. His ears had picked up a noise, a scrape of leather on wood, a footfall. Elizabeth.

"Did you know Caroline was asleep before I left the room?" A rustle of clothing, a hint of perfume, and something else. "Can I, uh, get you something to drink?"

Her voice. It was in her voice. Strained, uneasy, and he thought that even if she didn't say a word, he'd have picked up on it, for it created a tension in the air that he could feel as easily

as he felt the fabric on the couch. He needed
to tell her he felt as awkward as she. But for
now, he simply smiled and nodded his head.
"Iced tea, Coke, anything cold would be great,
Elizabeth."

"I'll just be a minute." He heard her leave
the room and felt the relief, heard the relief,
that rode each syllable. Thirsty or not, he'd
have asked for something, for both their sakes.

He tracked her by sound; cupboard door
opening and closing, fridge door opening and
closing, ice tinkling in a glass, the metallic
click of a pop top being snapped off, and the
gurgle of liquid being poured. And then her
footsteps, light and quick, bringing her back to
him.

"Here you are." Elizabeth placed the glass
in his hand, waited briefly for him to get a firm
grasp, then let go.

"Thank you." He patted the seat next to
him. "Come here, Elizabeth. Sit down."

She didn't answer but she sat. Carefully and
just far enough away so that their bodies didn't
touch. He smiled at that. And then he reached
out, groping for her hand, leaving her no
choice but to place her hand in his or watch
him scrabbling in the air. It was unfair, but he
did it anyway because he needed so badly to
touch her as well as to talk with her.

"Elizabeth—"

"Mac—"

"You go ahead . . . "

"Please, you first . . . "

Their joint laughter was spontaneous—and an icebreaker. And it helped ease the wave of emotion that clutched at his throat. She was here. He'd hardly been able to believe she'd offered to come. He'd expected concern, a card, some calls. But not this. And though he still wasn't comfortable about agreeing to it, he told himself she was an adult, responsible for her own decisions. It rang a little false in his ear but he was doing a bang-up job ignoring it. Besides, he knew exactly why *he* wanted her here. The real puzzler, as far as he was concerned, was why *she* came. His grip tightened on her hand. "Thank you for coming."

"I was happy to, Mac."

Of course she'd say that. How could she not? She was laboring under the assumption that either Kate would be worked to death or they'd be cast out on their own. It was time to clear the air. He'd gotten her here under false pretenses. There was no getting around it. And he couldn't have her here and not tell her. So, if coming clean sent her packing, so be it. He had to be able to live with himself. "Elizabeth, I need to tell you something."

"Yes?"

"I feel lousy saying this but here goes." He shrugged and sucked in a mouthful of air. "I had no business letting you take off work and come here to take care of us. See, what I didn't tell you or Kate was that I found someone, some woman through one of those agencies, I could hire to live in and help out. But when Kate told me what you'd offered, I . . . well, you know what I did. Nothing. I just let you tool on down here thinking you were our only hope. I'm really sorry, Elizabeth.''

He'd wanted *her*. Not someone from an agency. For a moment she felt buoyed up by a fantasy so illogical that she banished it immediately. Reason told her that what he'd really been concerned about was Caroline. A woman from an agency was an unknown entity—and given how he felt about his niece, it was no surprise to her that he'd be very reluctant about a stranger taking care of her. And no matter how she felt about Mac—and she wasn't about to deal with that—she herself would have come for the baby's sake alone. ''Please, don't apologize, Mac,'' she said. ''I wanted to come. And I was so glad that you let me. Besides, surely I'm better for Caroline than someone she doesn't know.''

''You're right.'' *And better for me as well though you don't know it.* Slowly, he loosened his tight grip, and with his thumb began to stroke her palm. For just this much he'd be content, and thank his lucky stars she wasn't going to leave.

Her fingers twitched in response to Mac's touch and she felt the heat climb her arm. She looked at her hand tucked into his, watched his broad thumb moving in slow and easy circles on her palm, and as the seconds slipped by, it dawned on her that he couldn't watch her watching. It had seemed so obvious he couldn't see that this aspect of it hadn't occured to her. And for the next few moments, she took full advantage of it.

She let her eyes roam where they would, from his head to his toes and back again. He had an athlete's body, well-muscled, tanned. But it was his hair, the color of mellow pine and in need of a trim, and the soft blond fuzz that covered his arms and legs, that made her fingers twitch. His nose had a small bump that made her think it'd been broken, his jaw was stubbled, and a strong pulse beat rythmically at his neck. But it was the bandages that reminded her of why she was here—and how right it felt to be back again.

And then he grinned.

"A penny for your thoughts." His voice was a humor-filled drawl. He raised the glass to his lips and drank deeply.

Elizabeth felt the rush of embarrassment heat her neck and face even as she told herself he couldn't possibly know she'd been staring at him like some voyeur. "I was thinking of lunch," she lied, and pulled her hand free of his. "I'm sure you must be hungry. It's way past noon. Why don't I get us something to eat?"

"I'd like that. But wait a minute. I want to tell you a little story." He reached out for her hand again and this time found it without her help.

"Yesterday, I was sitting around with Ted, Kate's oldest boy. We were just hanging out in the family room. He'd been playing with those Legos he likes and when I asked him what he wanted to ask me he said, 'But, Uncle Mac, how did you know I was going to ask you something? You can't see.' " He chuckled. "What do you think, Elizabeth? A sixth sense? Intuition?"

"Well . . . " She thought it was humiliating, that's what she thought. "I think," she sniffed defensively, " . . . you made a lucky guess." He chuckled and she watched that wide, mobile mouth spread in a silly grin and found herself chuckling too. "And you've done it again. You caught me red-handed, Mac."

"Maybe. And maybe I'm feeling a little envious because I sure wish I could see you right now."

"Oh, Mac." She reached out with her free hand and touched his cheek, the edge of the bandage. "The truth is I . . . I don't even know what to say, what to ask, or-or what to do."

She laid her hand against his cheek. "Are you in any pain?"

"No, Elizabeth, not a bit. It's the . . . the helplessness I feel." His voice was mocking as he raised the hand that held his glass. "I can probably put this down on the coffee table without much of a problem." He leaned forward and lowered the glass, missing the coffee table on the first two passes, but finding it on the third. He placed the glass too near the edge and Elizabeth flinched and started to reach for it, but something about Mac made her stop. His fingers slid down the glass and slowly he inched it further onto the table until it bumped into a stack of magazines. "There." He grunted with satisfaction. "But unless I have help, I can't get to the next room without tripping or knocking something over."

"That's why I'm here, Mac," she answered softly. This time she squeezed his hand and knew she'd been given at least one of the answers about why she was here. To be of help. To learn to help. There was a lump in her throat and goose bumps on her arms. For the first time in her life she felt needed. Truly needed.

"Sorry for the whining. I'm lucky and I know it," he said gruffly. "And if you're still offering a meal, I'll take it."

"I won't be a minute." She hurried out to the kitchen and as she layered meat and cheese on fresh rye bread, she thought of the kind of man he was. Open. Human. And unafraid. Able to let his frustrations and his fears show. She slathered on hot mustard, then went to the fridge to look for pickles.

He was also downright sneaky, Elizabeth decided, watching Mac settle himself down on the seat of the swing and, in the blandest of tones, ask her to sit next to him.

"I thought maybe I should tidy up the house a bit, Mac." She stood her ground, not moving an inch. Her voice was innocence itself.

"It was just done yesterday, Elizabeth. I had someone come in."

"Well, I could water the lawn."

He could hear the smile in her voice. "Not until sundown. Conserves water."

"Check on Caroline?"

"You just did."

"Walk the dog?"

"I lost the leash."

She grinned. Maybe this was what she'd missed the most. The teasing, the humor. "I could sweep the porch?"

"And make a sick man sneeze?"

"Well, I could . . ."

"Give up, admit you're licked."

"Never."

"Okay. Then pamper me, give me a little TLC. Can't you see I need it?"

"Like a hole in the head." She plunked down next to him, laughing. They were acting like teenagers. It should have been embarrassing. It felt invigorating. His arm came around her, his fingers curling at her shoulder, and she let him pull her close.

"You'd have made a terrible Florence Nightingale, you know." His voice was a low, comforting rumble at her ear.

"I could take a course."

"An excellent idea."

"But is there one available?"

"You're in luck. I heard there was."

"Wonderful. Where do I sign up?"

"Not far." His hand moved up and cupped her head. "Right here, in fact." And then, with an unerring sense of direction, he found her mouth: cool, petal-soft, and waiting.

It felt as though the earth was moving. It was only the swing.

It sounded like thunder. It was her heartbeat and his.

Her arms wound around his neck, his bandage tickled her nose, and her lips held his.

This man had opened her eyes, her mind, her heart. His scent was intoxicating, heady, imprinting itself bone-deep. The sound at the back of her throat was a purr of pleasure.

Her hair was springy beneath his palm, her lips tender and tempting. His senses reeled and spun like a top. There was no explaining this to himself. He'd tried. He'd thought long and hard. Not just chemistry, not simply caring or concern. Though there was passion, there was also peace. Of a sort. All he knew for sure was that he'd found what he'd wanted. Knew what he needed. But could it be his? *Should* it be?

The backfire of a car snapped them to attention like soldiers at roll call and brought Elizabeth to her feet. Her face flushed and heated as one of the passengers, in a car packed with teenagers, yelled, "Way to go, Coach!"

Mac laughed and raised his hand in a wave. "That sounds like David Brockman. He's my quarterback, a great athlete."

"Oh." Elizabeth was still recovering. They were sitting out there in broad daylight, kissing, for heaven's sake—and Mac waved! Just waved!

"It's okay, Elizabeth," he said. He turned his head toward her, toward the sound of her voice. He heard the discomfort, imagined her face was scarlet. Nothing new about that.

She sat back down next to him and took his hand in hers. It was okay, as he put it. It was not only okay, she was going to do it again. She leaned forward and touched his mouth with hers. . . .

Elizabeth tucked the sheet, as best she could, under the couch cushions. Mac and Caroline were both in bed, the house was locked up, the day nearly over. She plumped the pillow and lay down, pulling the sheet up to her chin.

It was a day she'd not soon forget. A day that made her feel proud. A day of work with no reward but the smiles of two people who needed her, who depended on her. She rolled onto her side and tucked her fist under her chin. Of course, the days were numbered. And then she'd leave.

Chapter Nine

Elizabeth slipped a new blade into the razor and laid it on the bathroom counter, mentally ticking off the wide assortment of skills she'd acquired since she'd first met Caroline and Mac. But barbering? Shaving a man? She chuckled softly, stepped out into the hall, and knelt by the swing.

"Never in my wildest dreams did I ever think I'd be shaving a man," she whispered to her niece.

The baby gurgled and squealed and Elizabeth nodded solemnly. "I'm glad you understand. Now, wish me luck. I'm off to get the barbarian who needs to be shorn!"

Of course, Caroline answered her. She had no trouble at all interpreting those baby noises.

141

And she was off to the kitchen to get the barbarian. She really was. But she was also fiddling, dragging her feet. She wasn't quite as brave as she'd led her niece to believe. Not that her sweetie really understood, of course, but pretending she had an understanding ally was a huge consolation. *Enough,* she told herself sternly. *Go get Mac and get the job done.* She squared her shoulders, took a deep breath, and plastered a smile on her face.

"I'm ready if you are, Mac," she said briskly as she entered the kitchen.

"I think I need my head examined," he groaned.

"Nope. Just a shave, that's all that head of yours needs." His hesitancy was the boost she needed for her flagging confidence. Grasping Mac by the hand, she led him out the door.

"With an electric razor."

"You told me you never use one."

"Now sounds like a good time to start."

"You don't have one."

"The stores open at ten. I can wait."

"I can't. You look terrible."

She stopped at the bathroom door and said, "I brought a chair in. I thought it might be more comfortable." He balked as she guided him to the chair and she laughed. "My goodness, I do believe you're scared."

"Try terrified." She settled a towel around his shoulders and he managed to grab her hand. "Do you have a license to do this, lady?"

Her smile was wicked. "All the license I need, mister. Lots of time and a very sharp razor."

But as she turned on the hot water, she squeezed her eyes shut and said a very fast prayer. She wouldn't let Mac know, but she was as frightened as he was.

Twenty minutes later, Elizabeth sighed with unfeigned relief and straightened up. "Done." She raised her arms above her head and stretched. Her neck had a crick in it and her lower back ached. Now she understood why barbers and beauticians used chairs whose height could be adjusted. Letting her arms fall back to her sides, she eyed Mac critically. "Not bad," she added. "If I do say so myself."

"Feels great." Mac rubbed his hand over his jaw. But he wasn't feeling too terrific. How could he? It was an ordeal to sit there with his hands clutched in his lap as Elizabeth's hands circled his jaw with a hot cloth, or as her fingers lathered on shaving cream. Her body kept brushing his and her scent nearly drove him crazy. He didn't know if he could go through this again. And it wasn't because she'd nicked him. In fact, not a drop of blood had been drawn.

"Does it, Mac? I hope so."

"You bet." She was standing behind him with her hands on his shoulders and he reached up, grabbed her hands, and pulled them down across his chest. It forced her to bend over, and as he knew it would, it brought her head next to his. Her hair tickled his neck; her breath was soft at his ear. Of course he'd go through this again. Maybe it was torture, but it was the sweetest kind. "I'll be back tomorrow, same time, okay?"

"I'll be here," she replied softly.

He held fast to her hands and turned his head a fraction more. She turned hers. Their lips touched, parted, then met again. What he wanted was all of her tomorrows.

Elizabeth glanced out of the corner of her eye at Mac who was slouched comfortably next to her on the couch, listening to the evening news on the radio. She slit open the cream-colored envelope with the familiar embossed name. Only the address was different. Italy, now. The stationery was scented, the handwriting looping and overdone. She read slowly, disbelievingly, and then read it again. Her hands dropped to her lap and the two sheets of vellum slid to the floor.

Mac heard the rustle of paper, heard Elizabeth's quick, indrawn breath, and sensed her distress. He reached over and flipped off the radio. "Elizabeth?"

It was a moment before she answered him and when she did, her voice was distant and cold. "Yes?"

It had been a long while since he'd heard those chilly tones. He eased his arm along the back of the couch, searching for her. "Can you tell me what's wrong?"

"Are you suggesting something is wrong?"

He flinched at her question and thought he'd have felt better if she'd slapped him in the face. She wasn't simply dismissing him, she wasn't even acknowledging his concern.

"I thought so," he answered flatly.

"Well, then, you were incorrect." She reached down and retrieved the letter from the floor, folded it carefully, and slid it back into the scented envelope.

"I see." He groped for the radio, found the knob, and turned it on.

"I'm going out on the porch for a while. Would you like to come?" Her voice was unfailingly polite. It was the last thing she wanted.

"Not right now, Elizabeth." He heard her leave the room, heard the door open and close. Propping his hands behind his head, he leaned back against the cushions. He hadn't heard one word of the news. Instead, he thought of the woman who'd left the room.

There were just two facts that he knew for sure. Her secretary had forwarded her mail. And something in the mail had disturbed her greatly. He wiggled his feet out of his shoes and stretched out his legs. Actually, he thought, he knew a little more than that. He knew he'd been hurt by her rebuff. And he knew he'd get over it. More important, he knew that her reaction—the distancing, the secretiveness—was how she'd always coped.

When the time was right, he'd do no cajoling. He'd confront her.

The news was over; some good blues music was starting. He had every intention of enjoying it. Until it was time for Elizabeth.

Elizabeth stood at the porch rail, her body rigid, her eyes unfocused, her mind whirling. Restlessly, she rocked back on forth on the balls of her feet. Normally she'd have gone for a run, a punishing ten-mile run, or headed for her athletic club and found someone to join her for a brutal, no-holds-barred game of racquetball. Her hands clutched the porch rail. She couldn't leave two helpless people alone.

Alone. A familiar word, a familiar feeling. She hated it, avoided it. She knew how to keep it at bay, could even bury it for long periods of time. The word continued to taunt her, mock her. It wheedled and whispered, promising nothing but pain. Where once it may have had validity, today it had none. It was destructive, destroying, and at this point in her life, mostly self-inflicted. The moon was shuttered by clouds banked high and dark. A breeze, the precursor of the coming summer storm, fingered its way through the foliage, cooled her hot skin, and lifted her spirits. It was time. Time to look within, to let others in.

Dry-eyed, dry-mouthed, she turned slowly toward the house, toward the light, the music, and Mac.

"Mac?"

"Yes, Elizabeth?" He pushed himself up and turned down the radio. Just that one word, his name, and he knew he wouldn't have to confront her. She was ready to confront herself.

"I'm sorry. I was so rude." That was the easy part, the apology. She sat carefully at the far end of the couch. More was needed, more required if she were to change the habits of a lifetime and face the ghosts of the past.

"It's okay." His voice was gentle and accepting. And it brought tears to her eyes.

"No. It's not. It's really not. Not anymore." She laced her fingers together. "I really don't know where to start. I don't know how to begin. . . ."

"Sure you do. You start at the beginning."

The beginning. She picked up the envelope and laid it in her lap. "I received a letter from my mother. It seems she's marrying again. A count this time. Or at least he claims to be." She stared at the familiar handwriting. "It's not the marriage; that's nothing new. . . . It's the lack of concern, the indifference." She snatched up the envelope and balled it in her hand. "I had a brother . . . a relative . . . family. She never told me until it was too late!" Her voice rose. "Do you know why she didn't tell me? Because when she married my father she deliberately cut off any communication with Michael's father. She had snagged a wealthy man and she didn't want a baby boy and an ex-husband to ruin her chances. My father died when I was two. She's been running through his money ever since." Her tears took her by surprise. Helpless to stop them, she finally gave up and let herself do what she hadn't done since she was a child. She let herself cry.

Mac groped on the table beside him for the box of tissues. It was high time Elizabeth grieved. Grieved for the mother-daughter relationship she'd never had, for the brother she'd never know. He wanted to curse the woman responsible, but couldn't. He pitied her instead.

Elizabeth took the box Mac held out. Every instinct she possessed urged her to leave— leave the room, this house, this man. She felt vulnerable, but more than that, worse than that—exposed. She dried her eyes, blew her nose, and put on her glasses. Mac just sat, as still and quiet as a Buddha. She wanted to be angry with him, even more so with herself. She sucked in a deep breath.

No! Not anymore! Shocked, her hand went to her mouth. Had she said that out loud? She swiveled her head and looked at Mac, then sighed. She had no way of telling. Not with the bandages on.

Bandages. That word, that single word, gave her the missing piece that had so eluded her. And it gave her the clarity she needed. Masks. She'd lived behind a mask for years. For protection, in denial, afraid of . . . afraid of what? Of being rejected, of being alone? Not good enough. It rang false. She'd made choices based on fears, old, old fears. And tonight, she was facing them, facing Mac, facing herself. She was no longer alone.

She spoke softly, picking her words carefully. "In her letter she didn't mention Caroline once! And I had sent her pictures and glowing descriptions. I just couldn't understand. I felt so angry." Her laugh was low and wry. "But I realize, now, that she probably hasn't even received my package. She doesn't know she has a grandchild because in her letter she says she's been traveling with this . . . this man for weeks. I was so angry, so upset, I wasn't thinking straight."

His hands were in his lap, palms up. They were large hands, strong and callused. She reached for the one closest to her and clasped it between her own. "And I guess I'd conjured up a little fantasy for myself that somehow once my mother found out she had a grandchild she would . . . oh, I don't know, be thrilled, come home, change somehow. I can't expect that. It's not fair to either her or me. I guess what's most important is I know what a difference Caroline has made in my life.''

''I know she has,'' he answered. His smile was inward, for he didn't want her to mistake it or misunderstand. Did she grasp, he wondered, how much she was changing, how she'd become willing to change? He wanted to take her in his arms and tell her how proud he was of her and how much it meant to him to have earned her trust. But he wouldn't take the chance. He wasn't even sure he had the right.

The rumble and roll of thunder was still distant, but the wind had picked up and the rain had begun. The storm was coming, was close. Yet for her, Elizabeth thought, it was as if the sun had come out. Her eyes rested on Mac.

She longed to wrap her arms around his neck.

She longed to tell him more . . . to tell him she thought she was falling in love with him.

But being her friend, having him as a friend, was something she didn't want to lose. Even knowing that there was some sort of chemistry between them, an attraction she couldn't deny, didn't mean she could expect his love.

Mac heard another clap of thunder and the sudden fury of the rain beating at the windows. Next to him, Elizabeth stirred.

''I'll just check on Caroline,'' she said.

"Okay. And you may want to get out candles and a flashlight in case the power goes out."

She squeezed his hand and stood. "All right. And Mac?"

"Yes?"

"Thank you for listening."

"Elizabeth, don't you understand you never have to thank me?"

Her footsteps were hurried and quick as she left the room. She couldn't have answered him if she'd wanted to.

The power didn't go out until Elizabeth was settled on her makeshift bed on the couch. She wouldn't have known if she hadn't been wide awake and had left the hall light on in case she'd have to get up in the middle of the night.

She stared into the darkness and thought of her conversation with Mac, a conversation that had remained on her mind all evening. She couldn't make excuses for her mother, but neither could she condemn her. Maybe she could forgive her—for she finally realized that her mother, whether she knew it or not, was paying a terrible price.

Rolling onto her side, she closed her eyes. Then bolted straight up. She'd set the clock radio so she'd be up in plenty of time to get Mac to his doctor's appointment. She fell back on the couch, laughing. How could she have forgotten the living, breathing alarm snuggled in her crib in the next room?

The storm raged outside as Elizabeth drifted off to sleep, with her last conscious thought of Mac—and the peace he was helping her find.

Mac edged open the door that led from the treatment rooms into the patient reception area and got his first good look at Elizabeth and Caroline. Perhaps the dark sunglasses dimmed their bright heads, shadowed their features; perhaps all color was a little distorted. None of that mattered, for he could see—and what he saw brought a lump to his throat the size of a softball. His girls. One he could claim, one he couldn't. It wasn't the way he wanted it. If the nurse hadn't come up behind him, wishing him well, talking about a follow-up appointment, he might have stood there forever.

Elizabeth heard Mac's voice and jerked upright. Despair dropped like a stone in her heart. The book dropped to the floor and her grip tightened on her niece's tummy. ''Oh, Mac.'' She rose unsteadily. He was grinning ear to ear and walking right toward her. ''Your bandages are off!'' She forced herself to sound cheerful. ''How . . . how wonderful!''

''Yep. I healed up a lot quicker than the doc thought I would.'' He leaned down and bussed Cappy on top of her head. ''Hey squirt,'' he said softly. And then he raised his head a fraction and looked at Elizabeth. "Who's the pretty lady you've got with you?"

"Oh, Mac." She smiled her answer, blushing like a schoolgirl. And before she had time to think he'd wrapped his arms around the two of them and kissed her. Kissed her hard and fast and with a kind of hunger that echoed in the deep sigh that followed.

"Let's get out of here, okay?"

"Don't forget your appointment card, Mr. McAllister." The receptionist was hanging over the counter waving at them.

With Cappy on his shoulder and an arm wrapped around Elizabeth, he went to the woman and took the card.

"My goodness!" The receptionist looked at Caroline and Elizabeth. "Why, that baby is just the spitting image of you, honey." She shot a simpering smile at Mac, then winked at Elizabeth. "I'll bet that makes Daddy real happy."

Her dislike of the woman was instant and alarming. Taken off guard, Elizabeth opted for bluntness. "Mac's not her father. He's her uncle."

"Oh . . . I see." The woman's eyebrows shot up and she looked at Mac as if he was the devil himself. "Well, never mind," she said, ignoring Mac and speaking directly to Elizabeth, her voice heavy with undertones of pity.

"Mommy and baby are just two peas in a pod, aren't you?"

Out of the corner of her eye, Elizabeth saw Mac's lips quirk up. He wasn't going to say a word! Leaning forward, she smiled ever so sweetly and said in a stage whisper calculated to titilate, "I'm not her mother." Turning to Mac, she asked blandly, "Are you ready to leave?"

Mac had all he could do not to burst out laughing. The receptionist's face was mottled with self-righteous indignation and Elizabeth's was pale with fury. Between the two of them there was enough heat to boil water. He couldn't get her out of there fast enough. "Sure am," he replied. Elizabeth flew out the door before he and Cappy were halfway across the room.

Slamming the car door shut, Elizabeth belted herself in. Mac had fastened Caroline into her carseat and was settling himself next to her. He had a big, goofy grin on his face that infuriated her. "I fail to see what's so funny," she snapped. "That woman was obnoxiously nosy!"

"I agree."

"Well," she huffed, not quite ready to let go, "of course, you didn't say one word!"

"I thought you said enough for the both of us, Elizabeth."

His chuckle was deep, full-throated, and just what she needed. Laughter welled and bubbled at the back of her throat. "Maybe. But it was none of her business."

"You're right. It wasn't."

He was almost too agreeable, too amiable. Defensively, she added, "Well, we aren't Caroline's mother . . . and father." Her laughter sputtered, died, and her voice utterly failed her.

"That we aren't."

Elizabeth kept her eyes focused on the road and tried to ignore the funny sort of throb she'd heard in Mac's voice and the hard knot just below her rib cage. The silence between them lengthened and she tried desperately to think of something neutral enough to talk about. She found her answer as she noticed a group of low brick buildings just ahead on her left. "What are those buildings?" she asked.

"Our community college. It's a pretty good little school. A lot of my kids go there for two years then transfer. They save a lot of money that way." He seemed as desperate as she to keep the conversation off themselves. "And they've got a lot of older students too. Especially women who want to go back to work after raising families or moms trying to get off welfare."

"Is that right?" She managed a quick glance at the campus as they passed by. While the buildings were architecturally nondescript, the wide lawns and towering trees lent a certain serenity. And what Mac had told her about the student body, especially the women. . . . It shocked her to realize she'd never thought of what it would be like to try to get an education with children to worry about. But the subject of mothers was one she didn't wish to pursue. She gripped the wheel tightly as her niece began to make fussy little noises, each one a decibel higher and louder.

Caroline, her face scrunched in misery, wailing like a banshee, would never understand how her outraged and indignant wails were exactly the distraction her aunt and uncle needed.

Chapter Ten

The tray in her hand forgotten, Elizabeth gazed out the kitchen window at Mac and Caroline. She had suggested an early lunch. Mac had suggested a picnic in the backyard. So while Elizabeth had fed Caroline, Mac had hauled out the playpen and an old blanket and put them in the shade of the maple tree. They'd eaten sandwiches, made small talk, and played with the baby. Now Caroline was lying in the playpen looking sleepy, and Mac was sitting yoga-style on the blanket, reading the paper, happy as a kid with a new toy. The dog had joined them and lay at Mac's side, her nose between her paws.

The bandages were off. The doctor was pleased; Mac was ecstatic; it was cause for celebration. *Then why is it,* she asked herself for the tenth time in as many minutes, *that such good news feels so bad?*

She put the tray down and gathered up the paper plates and napkins and tossed them in the trash, set the glasses in the sink, and then stopped. Stopped the fussing, the fiddling with glasses, and a baby bottle, and leftover grapes, and rested her hands on the cool Formica counter. Dust motes hung in the band of sunlight that streamed in the window, spilling across the floor, climbing the table leg. Sounds receded into the background and in the sunstruck silence she heard the voice in her head, answering the question she'd been asking herself over and over.

Because it's time now for you to leave.

She lifted her head and her eyes moved to the scrubbed table with the bright flowered placemats she'd laid out this morning. Her purse was there too, and a baseball glove of Mac's, a new one he'd worked on yesterday with a special oil he'd told her would make it soft and supple. Nudged up against the glove was a buttercup-yellow rattle. Her hands balled into fists and she shut her eyes, blocking out the visual reminders of Mac and Caroline. But it couldn't block out how she felt.

She'd fallen in love with her niece almost from the first moment she'd held her. With Mac, it'd been slower, more subtle, catching her unaware, like magic, dizzying and dazzling her. She felt a burning at the back of her throat. She could so easily say ''I love you'' to her niece. But not with Mac.

She suspected she was trying to make a little magic herself, trying to make more of attraction, of companionship, than was there. It was dangerous to confuse reality with illusion. She needn't hurt herself or others. She had a niece and a friend, a good friend. She'd leave it at that.

Her fingers unfolded and she opened her eyes. She'd pack after lunch, be gone before dinner. And most important, she'd stay out of Mac's arms.

And then the phone began to ring, shrill and loud.

Mac laid down the newspaper and stretched out full-length on the blanket. He could hear the soft, moist sounds of Cappy sucking her thumb. In a minute or two she'd be asleep. And in a minute or two Elizabeth would return and sit down beside him. He laced his hands behind his head. He no longer had a legitimate reason to have Elizabeth sit down beside him. That ended this morning in the doctor's office.

He let his thoughts drift back to the day Elizabeth had walked into his life, and grinned just thinking about it. Haughty, high-handed, cold as hoarfrost. Until she'd picked up her niece and dangled her on her lap. He knew it was his Cappy who'd first touched Elizabeth's heart.

His fingers plucked idly at the blades of grass at the edge of the blanket. And had he touched her heart as well? That was the question nagging at him like a sore tooth. That and his own heart.

For Pete's sake, McAllister. He was lying here in the grass like some love-struck teenage kid. This wasn't sensible, reasonable, the sign of a sane man. But love wasn't any of those things. He knew that all too well. He'd been taught by a little bit of a thing with a couple of teeth and dimpled knees.

So. He was going to tell Elizabeth that he'd fallen in love with her.

He was going to tell her that he needed her.

He was going to leave Cappy out of it because he'd never been looking for a mother for his niece and he wasn't now.

He was going to ask her to marry him, to be his wife.

Not because he thought she'd accept.

But because he'd never be able to live with himself if he didn't take the risk.

The phone snapped her out of her reverie and Elizabeth lifted the receiver. "Hello."

"Hello. Elizabeth? Is that you? This is Peggy." Her voice was barely above a whisper.

"Peggy? Hi. You'll have to speak up. I can't hear you."

"I can't speak up. Just try to listen, okay?"

There was an urgency in her secretary's voice that puzzled her. "What's the matter, Peggy? Are you all right?"

"I'm fine. It's you that—Oops, there's someone coming! Listen, please!" Her words came out in a breathy, panicked rush. "It's about your promotion. Oh, I'm so sorry, Elizabeth. I shouldn't be telling you something like this over the phone, but I don't know what else to do. You didn't get it. You didn't get the promotion."

Elizabeth heard someone in the background calling out a greeting to her secretary and then Peggy said, with great formality, "I'm sorry. I'll have to get back to you on that matter. Good-bye."

The dial tone buzzed before the recording came on reminding her that if she wished to make a call she needed to hang up and try again.

And then the beeping began, incessant, insistent—and unnoticed.

The phone finally had gone dead. It hung from its coiled cord like a spider dangling from its thread. The room was dim and shadowless as rooms were in the blind bright daytime of summer. Elizabeth sat slumped in a chair.

Small sounds crept into the stunned silence: the rhythmic tick of the wall clock, the hum of the refrigerator, her own shallow breathing.

The backdoor slammed and Mac strode into the kitchen with Caroline tucked in his arm. ''I thought I'd put shortstuff in her bed. She—'' Elizabeth's head came up and the look he saw in her eyes raised the hair on the back of his neck. ''I'll just put Cap down and be right back.''

His receding footsteps beat in her skull like a drum. She lifted her hands then let them fall back into her lap. *''I'm so sorry, Elizabeth . . . I shouldn't be telling you . . . You didn't get it.''* Peggy's voice had been a throaty whisper. *''You didn't get it. . . . ''*

Mac heard her sob, and it stopped him dead in his tracks at the kitchen door. Elizabeth sat hunched forward, her feet on the upper rung of the chair, her arms wrapped around her legs, her face buried between her knees. Her glasses sat on the sink. The tray was on the counter; the phone was off the hook.

It took him less than a second to make his decision. Quietly, he backed up, away from the kitchen. He closed the front door behind him without making a sound. His sunglasses slipped a little as he went down the steps and around the side of the house to the backyard. His mouth twisted in a half smile as he pushed the glasses back up the bridge of his nose. *Oh,*

Elizabeth. He crossed the backyard in angry, long strides, jerked open the shed door, and pulled out the lawn mower.

There was an ache in his chest and a ruthless impatience he'd have to wrestle with—for he was going to leave her alone. Until she wanted to come to him.

The sound of the mower brought her out of the chair and to the kitchen window. *Oh, Mac.* It was deliberate. He was leaving her alone to make her own decision, her own choices. If she wanted to talk to him, he'd be there. He would leave it entirely up to her.

She turned away from the window, away from the man in sunglasses and a baseball cap, pushing a lawn mower across the thick, sun-drenched grass.

So she could go to him. She would go to him.

She didn't get as far as the back porch. *You can't tell him!* The thought struck her like a blow to her body. She couldn't—for she wouldn't risk having him feel responsible, in any way, for her loss of the promotion.

Not that he was. Not that he ever could be. She paced the house with a restless, pent-up energy as her anger grew. What had Philip said just before she'd left to come help Mac? *"I think I see a pattern developing, Elizabeth. And I don't like it."*

He didn't like it? All those years, all those long hours. Not that Philip appreciated it, nor had she expected him to, for they had both worked at the same frenetic, formidable pace.

She came to a standstill as it suddenly occurred to her that Philip had a family, a wife, two boys. There was a photograph of them on his desk; it'd been there for years. He'd never discussed them; she'd never laid eyes on a one of them. It shocked her to realize he must be a stranger to them.

She felt a wash of unease, of discomfort, the sort of feeling that came when you saw yourself in another.

She hesitated at Caroline's room and then quietly opened the door. Her niece was sound asleep in a nest of stuffed animals, her mop of bright curls like a miniature orange-gold sun on her pillow. Elizabeth's hand froze in midair as she reached out for the doorknob.

You would've missed this, a small voice whispered.

Her hand was trembling as she shut the door. The words spun in her head as she resumed pacing, drinking in the small details, the slivers and slices of Mac's life: A wall covered with photographs of children in huddled, happy groups or lined up in triple rows, beaming with team pride. A few of Mac in football gear from college days and his year in the pros, a card table covered with flies and lures and an old fishing creel, a baseball bat sharing a corner with a broom, a stack of books by a chair, a cardboard box stuffed with paint-splattered coveralls and a pair of boots, a large collection of tapes and CDs piled next to the stereo adorned by a football, and everywhere, in every room, some reminder of his niece.

She came back to the kitchen window and saw Mac, drenched in sweat and sun, pushing the mower from one end of the yard to the other. Not just a jock, but a man, a caring, loving man who had a life—off the ballfield, outside of a gym.

He'd missed nothing.

And, for once, neither had she.

She left the kitchen and went to pack.

After hauling the suitcases out to her car and dumping them in the trunk, Elizabeth went back through the house to the kitchen. She'd heard the mower cut off, heard Mac come in.

He was standing by the table, red-faced, sweat-soaked, gulping down a glass of water. He turned toward her as she entered and her stomach lurched but she kept her face composed.

''Hello, Mac.''

''Elizabeth.'' His eyes narrowed. She sounded calm, collected, in control. But there was a pinched look around her nose and mouth and she was holding herself too stiffly, as if she might shatter if she moved too much—or was touched. Her eyes met his and he flinched. Their expression bruised from shock, they gave her away completely, though he doubted she knew it.

As she'd packed she'd rehearsed her lines; what she would say and more important what she wouldn't say. She was numb, numbed. The news had been devastating, but keeping it from Mac was as painful as an open wound. If she could ever tell him, would he understand? "About that phone call, Mac...there's a problem at the office. I'm sorry, but I'll have to get back right away."

"Of course." He set his glass carefully on the table. The mowing had given him time to think, to reflect. If it'd been a death or illness he was certain she would've told him. So he knew it would be her job.

"I don't...your bandages are—" She raised her hands helplessly. She couldn't find the words to express that she needed to leave but if his bandages hadn't been removed, she'd be staying, no matter what. She wondered if he'd even believe her.

"Elizabeth, it's all right." His fingers twitched with the urge to reach out for her, to haul her into his arms. What he needed to do— had to do—was let her go. No questions, no discussion, nothing.

Someone banged on the front door and they both turned toward the sound as Jake's familiar voice boomed through the house. "Hey, Mac. Where are you?"

They walked silently and in tandem to the living room where Jake stood waiting, propped on crutches. He greeted Elizabeth as awkwardly as a schoolboy and Mac with astonishment that his bandages were off so quickly.

Both of them gave Jake their undivided attention: Elizabeth inquiring about the progress of Jake's injuries, Mac answering Jake's questions about his eyes. Neither one looked at the other. Elizabeth checked her watch discreetly. Mac made the first move.

"What time were you planning on leaving, Elizabeth?" He was elaborately polite.

"In just a few minutes. I know Caroline is asleep, but I'll just tiptoe in and see her before I go."

"I hope you'll be coming back soon, Elizabeth," Jake said and winked. "Mac did nothing but talk about you after you left last time."

Elizabeth's eyes flew to Mac's then back to Jake's. She couldn't read Mac's face. Jake's was a different matter. "Well . . . I'll just go see Caroline."

Mac couldn't help but see the humor. Elizabeth was embarrassed; Jake was oblivious to the strain between them. And himself? Something was gnawing at him that he couldn't quite get a hold on yet. Asking Jake to stay put, he followed Elizabeth to Cappy's room.

Elizabeth hung over the crib rail. Her niece lay on her back, a dimpled arm flung above her cap of curls, the other resting on the back of a fuzzy bear. Her eyelashes lay on her rounded cheeks like tiny fans and her mouth moved in a small, involuntarily motion, shaping itself into a smile. Elizabeth's heart couldn't have felt fuller—or heavier. "Good-bye, sweetheart." She barely breathed the words as she reached out and touched the silky-soft hair.

Mac watched from the doorway and couldn't stop the instant flashback to the first time he'd seen Elizabeth in this room with his Cappy. And dismissed it abruptly. *Get on with it, Mc-Allister,* he told himself.

"Can I get your bags?"

Her knuckles showed white as they clutched the crib. It was time to go. She turned and walked to the door, to Mac standing with arms folded across his chest, his eyes somber and watchful. "I've already taken them to the car." She spoke quietly, afraid to wake the baby.

His eyebrows rose but he said nothing, just turned on his heel and walked to the front door.

"Good-bye, Jake." With a smile that actually pained her, Elizabeth acknowledged Jake's breezy wave of farewell and moved hurriedly through the room and out the door Mac held open for her.

She heard Mac's footsteps behind her on the porch stairs. Somehow, before she made it to the car, he got ahead of her and swung open the door.

"Thanks for coming and helping me out, Elizabeth."

"I was happy to, Mac." His arm was laid casually across the top of the car door. His body blocked her from getting in. She pushed at her glasses and frowned. "May I get in?"

"Yep." She took a step forward. He shook his head. He knew what the gnawing in his gut was about. He needed to let her go—he also needed to speak. "But not just yet, honey. Not until you've heard what I need to say."

Honey. His endearment shocked her more than his refusal to let her get in her car. And then the memory of the phone call returned, and with it an anguish and vulnerability so huge it made her feel exposed. She had to leave, to get away. "Mac, please. Not now."

"Yes, now." His voice was harsh, his eyes hard. "There are just two things I want to say. And I'll be brief. The first is this—when and if you want to talk, I'll be here." He grabbed her by the shoulder and none too gently pushed her into the car.

Leaning in, he cupped her chin in his hand. "And the second is that—" His mouth came to hers, swiftly, without apology, and overpowering. ''I love you, Elizabeth Margaret Kincaid.''

The car door closed with a solid thunk and then he was gone.

Elizabeth had no idea how many minutes had passed, only that it was unbearably hot. Beads of perspiration rolled down her face and neck; the air was suffocating and thick. Her hand shook as she stuck the key in the ignition and started the car.

Chapter Eleven

Two weeks had passed. Two lousy, loused-up weeks and not a word from Elizabeth. He couldn't look at Cappy and not think of her. He couldn't water those stupid flowers she'd planted and not want to send her a bunch. He hadn't had a decent night's sleep since she'd taken off.

He shoved his wallet into the back pocket of his khakis, picked up his keys, and left the house. He'd made his decision last night and had taken Cappy to Kate's at seven this morning. Sliding into the car, he flipped on the ignition and pulled away from the curb. It was eight A.M. on the button. It was going to hit ninety-five degrees. He was going to the city. He was going to find Elizabeth.

*   *   *

Elizabeth woke slowly. No alarm awakened her. Just morning sounds, cars passing, birds tittering, and a good night's sleep. The first in two weeks. She sat up slowly and looked at the clock. Ten A.M. Normally, she'd have been up by six. Her eyes went to the photograph of Mac and Caroline she'd propped against her lamp. He'd said he loved her. She hoped he meant it. She padded barefoot to the kitchen to make coffee. She would leave in a couple of hours. She was going to find Mac—and tell him she loved him.

Mac stepped out of the elevator and crossed the hall. The bunch of flowers in his hand were already starting to wilt. He'd been sent up, after a discreet telephone call, to meet with Elizabeth's secretary. He was familiar with layers of protection but this scenario had a different feel to it—too secretive, too suspicious.

A young woman with shiny black hair pulled severely back looked up as he walked across the thick wool carpeting. He kept the hand that held the flowers behind his back.

"Peggy? I'm Mac McAllister."

"Mr. McAllister."

Mac's smile faded. There was something wrong with this lady. Her eyes were troubled, her voice unfriendly, and his name meant nothing to her. "I'm looking for Elizabeth Kincaid.'' His eyes strayed to the closed door behind the secretary.

''I'm sorry, she's not here.''

''Can you tell me when she'll be back?''

''No, I cannot.''

''Look, miss, I'm a friend of hers and I've driven all morning to get here and I'm not leaving until I see her.''

''Then you'll have a very long wait, sir. She no longer works here.''

''What?'' Mac's voice was a roar and the secretary flattened herself against the chair, her eyes wide with fright.

''I'm sorry.'' Mac leaned toward the woman, who showed no sign of trusting him. ''I didn't mean to scare you.'' He shrugged helplessly. ''I didn't know.'' For a moment he stood there, staring at the closed door, then spun around and walked rapidly out of the room.

He didn't notice the tears in Peggy's eyes or see her hand reach for the phone.

Elizabeth heard the phone ringing as she got out of the shower. She let it ring and chuckled when she remembered she'd turned the answering machine off last night. Let them call back, she thought. The only person she wanted to talk to today wouldn't be calling her—but she'd be talking to him before nightfall.

Toweling herself dry, she slipped into a short cotton kimono and went to the bedroom. She pulled out a sundress and rummaged for sandals. She dressed quickly, brushed her hair, skimmed her lips with gloss, and added a touch of mascara. Gathering her heavy hair at the back of her neck, she fastened on a barrette and stuck her glasses on her nose. She found her purse and keys, and opened a shopping bag she'd laid on her bureau. The baseball cap was new and stiff and had the logo of Mac's old football team on the front. She pushed it firmly down on the crown of her head, grinned at herself in the mirror, and nearly danced to the front door.

Mac squealed to a stop in front of the brick town house and checked the address. This was it. He scanned the street looking for a parking place, saw one behind him about half a block away, and backed up, oblivious to the car that swung out, horn blaring, to avoid rear-ending him. Nosing his car into the slot, he picked up the bunch of flowers, climbed out of the car, and stood transfixed.

It was Elizabeth coming out the front door. There was no question about it. He'd come barrelling into the city and hunted her down because there were one or two questions he'd wanted to ask her. A smile spread, slow and easy, across his face and he started to walk toward Elizabeth—a most peculiar question now uppermost in his mind.

Elizabeth ran down the stairs to her car and bent to the door lock, humming beneath her breath.

Mac moved fast, but quietly. Keeping to the street, he came up behind her and, reaching out, snaked his arms around her waist and pulled her back against him. "Where'd you get the good-looking cap, Elizabeth?"

Her keys clattered to the sidewalk; her squeal brought startled glances from passersby. She recognized the voice, the silly, crazy, wonderful voice, even as she shrieked. His arms loosened their grip as she twisted around to face him. "Mac, you nearly scared me to death!"

Her glasses had slipped to the tip of her nose, her cap was askew, and her lips were twitching as she tried in vain to keep from smiling.

"You didn't answer my question." He wrapped his arms around her and pulled her close.

"What? Oh!" She started to laugh. "At a sporting goods store. Do you like it?"

"I don't know. You'll have to look up." She raised her head as he lowered his. The bill of her cap caught him under the nose and he grunted. Plucking it off her head, he bunched it into the hand that held the flowers and brought his mouth next to hers. "Can I decide later?"

"Umm, I guess so." She laid her hand against his cheek. "Is there something you want first?"

"Yes. You could say that." His eyes held hers as their lips met and his chest swelled with emotion. What he saw in those blue, blue eyes gave him all the answers he needed.

And then, in the noisy, hot bustle of a workday morning, leaning against Elizabeth's car, they kissed.

Mac whispered at her ear. "Where were you off to, Elizabeth?"

"To find the man I loved."

"I better not keep you, then." He gave her a playful shove.

"Oh, I hope you do." She tilted her head back and looked him straight in the eye. "Because you're the man I love."

"I love you too, sweetheart." He pulled her back into his arms. "That's what I came to tell you."

Mac's mouth captured hers and Elizabeth was certain she could hear the hum of her pulse and the thud of Mac's heart. The blare of horns and rude shouts finally got their attention.

"We're going to get hit if we don't move." Mac wrapped his arm protectively around her shoulder.

"And I think we're making a spectacle of ourselves." Elizabeth pushed Mac back and closed the car door. "Come on," she said.

At the top of the stairs just before she opened the door, Mac plopped the baseball cap back on her head and thrust the bouquet of flowers into her hand.

"They looked great when I picked them this morning." The drooping, wilted flowers were already turning brown around the edges.

"I'll bet they did." She laughed as she raised them to her nose.

"I know a place where you could pick them fresh every day."

"You do?" Smiling, she unlocked the door and swung it open. "Why don't you come in and tell me about it?"

An hour later, he'd more than explained and enlightened her. Elizabeth sighed and nestled closer to Mac's side. She smiled as she looked at their feet propped on the coffee table. It wasn't quite the same, she thought. They were missing a baby, a dog, and popcorn, but it was close. She nudged the baseball cap that lay on the table with her toe as Mac squeezed her shoulder.

"Are you ready to tell me what happened, Elizabeth?"

"Yes." She sat forward, out of the circle of his arm, and picked up her cap. "Can I tell you in the car? There's a baby I want to see."

"Absolutely."

Five miles out of town, she told him about the promotion she'd lost.

"Oh, Elizabeth. I'm sorry."

"I'm not. Apparently I needed something cataclysmic to get my attention. When I resigned last week, I kissed Phillip and thanked him." She chuckled. "I don't think he's recovered yet."

He swiveled his head and looked at her. "Elizabeth, I hope you aren't trying to put up some kind of brave front."

How like him to want to be sure. "No, Mac," she replied. She laid her hand against the back of his neck. "Do you know what helped me the most?"

He shook his head.

"My mother."

He remained silent, waiting, giving her all the time she'd need.

"I have a picture of her sitting on a balcony with the ocean behind her. The ocean is this gorgeous blue-green and the sky is cloudless. She looks lovely, of course, elegant. And unhappy. It seems as if she's completely unaware of the beauty behind her."

She squinted out the window. Heat waves rippled across the highway; the air inside the car was cool. She inhaled deeply and continued. "The picture was on my desk. When I returned, I went into my office, sat at my desk, and looked at that photograph. It was like seeing myself. There's a window behind me, a world outside that window. I'd never bothered to turn around and look.''

They were at the town limits and in minutes they'd be at Kate's house and she'd be able to hold Caroline in her arms. ''You know, Mac, it was as if there were bars on that window. I'd gotten a glimpse of life. But I didn't know how to get out.'' Her voice dropped and the tears that had filmed her eyes slid soundlessly down her cheeks. ''I was afraid to get out.''

''I know you were, honey.'' Mac pulled the car into Kate's driveway. ''Stay right here. I'll be out in a second.''

''What about Kate? I don't want to be rude.''

''She'll understand, I promise you.''

Elizabeth heard his voice choke. And she was almost certain his eyes looked wet.

Elizabeth sat on the porch swing with Caroline snuggled in her lap. Mac stood at the top of the stairs. ''Don't you girls go anywhere. I'll be right back.'' He ran down the stairs and disappeared around the side of the house.

Five minutes later he was back and sat down beside Elizabeth and Caroline. ''Elizabeth.'' He pulled her left hand from the baby's tummy and held it tight. ''Will you marry me?''

''Yes, Mac. I will,'' she answered softly.

Reaching into his shirt pocket, he pulled out a small flower. It was a cornflower, a beautiful, deep blue, with a stem he'd tied into a circle. "I'm sorry this isn't a diamond, sweetheart."

"Oh, Mac. I've never wanted a diamond."

He slipped the flower onto her finger and grinned. "Well, it sure matches your eyes."

Caroline wiggled impatiently and made a long series of adorable sounds.

"Absolutely, pipsqueak. Your eyes too." Mac laughed.

Elizabeth held out her hand with the funny little flower bedecking her finger. Of course, she understood every word Caroline said.

And it seemed Mac did too.

Epilogue

Her office was cool, the sun a July white-hot. Elizabeth gazed out the window from her desk. She was still clasping the letter in her hand. Her mother would arrive next week. It would be her second visit. The first had been for Elizabeth's wedding last October. She'd come with a title, a gift for her grandchild Caroline, and two cases of a French mineral water she drank exclusively.

Elizabeth slipped the letter into her purse and gathered up her folders. Though there'd been no heart-to-heart chats and much was left unsaid, Elizabeth was grateful for what there was. And her mother was bringing the Count this time—she'd said he simply had to be with

181

her to celebrate the birth of her second grand-child.

Standing, Elizabeth walked to the window. Waddled is more like it, she thought with a smile as she rubbed the small of her back. The campus was quiet this afternoon: no students lounging under the trees or ambling along the wide paths. The heat had driven everyone inside.

Except for two very familiar people, cutting across the grass from the parking lot. She folded her arms across her stomach and felt the baby kick. Instinctively, she rocked a little, comforting the bit of life inside her. The Mutt-and-Jeff pair were making their way very slowly toward her building. It stood to reason, of course. Someone under two feet tall took very tiny steps. And someone well over six feet had to be very, very patient.

Elizabeth turned her back on the window and went out the door—to meet her husband and first child.